HE ALONE DEFIED THE COSMIC VAMPIRES!

When the outlawed scientist Jim Hunt leaped from the prison plane, he had no suspicion that he was not the only one falling silently through the midnight sky. But other, stranger exiles were landing at that very moment in the same backwoods region . . . exiles from the unknown depths of outer space, exiles seeking human food.

When Jim started to make his way back home, he discovered the full horror of that night's events. For the people he met had become mere flesh-and-blood puppets, mindless creatures doing the bidding of the unseen invaders. And though every man's hand was against him, both free and enslaved, Jim knew that he alone was humanity's only hope for survival.

Murray Leinster's BRAIN-STEALERS is an unusually gripping science-fiction novel of thought transference, invaders from space, and vampirism on a world-wide scale!

Turn this book over for second complete novel.

Something about the author:

Will F. Jenkins, better known to readers under his popular pen-name of *Murray Leinster,* has been entertaining the public with his exciting fiction for several decades. Called by some the dean of modern science-fiction, he was writing these amazing super-science adventures back in the early twenties before there ever was such a thing as an all-fantasy magazine. His short stories, novelettes, and serial novels appeared in most of the major American magazines, both slick and pulp, and many have been reprinted in various languages all over the world. He has made a distinguished name for himself (or rather two names!) in the fields of adventure, western, historical, sea, and suspense stories.

Among his recent science-fiction books have been *The Last Space Ship, Space Platform,* and an anthology *Great Stories of Science Fiction.* A thrilling novel of another dimensional world entitled GATEWAY TO ELSEWHERE was published by ACE Books earlier this year.

The BRAIN-STEALERS is his latest imaginative adventure and one of his most unusual.

The

Brain - Stealers

BY
MURRAY LEINSTER

ACE BOOKS, INC.
23 West 47th Street   New York 36, N. Y.

1

THE SPACE-CRAFT landed. Silently. Gently. In deep forest. Within it there was venom and dissension. Silent venom. Soundless dissension. Thoughts. Only thoughts. A thought of bitter reproach—for gluttony. A thought of furious defensiveness. Angry, soundless accusations and counter-accusations. Then a cold, hard thought, reporting fact. The air outside the ship was good and the temperature bearable. There would be animals. Because of—the thought was icily savage, and meant gluttony—they would have to move of themselves, rather than be carried as was more convenient. But half a dozen of them should be able to handle any single animal on a strange world. There must be, though, no—again the savage thought of gluttony—until they had learned the nature of life on this world. Until they had some idea of its more intelligent and useful forms.

The craft that had landed was not large. Where it rested amid huge forest patriarchs, the branches had swerved aside and closed above it. It was hidden from above. But speckles of moonlight penetrated the leaves. They showed, presently, a circular slab in the ship's side in the act of unscrewing. It was a door.

Presently the moonlight shone upon movement. Upon movements. Creatures in awkward, unaccustomed self-locomotion. They were very small, compared to men, and their appearance was extremely improbable. They hobbled painfully in a compact group. At first they did not communicate even with each other, as if they strained whatever senses they possessed in the effort to savor the nature of this strange planet. Then the thoughts began. They expressed disgust. Disdain.

Then the icy, cold, clear thought that here the ground was firm and the vegetation worn away, is if by the passage of many animals.

The hobblings went along the path. Presently there was a light. An artificial light. There was tumultuous interchange of thought at ground-level among the struggling, painfully un-adept pedestrians. They moved forward. A dog barked furiously and rushed at them.

The small creatures stood still. The dog slowed, and stopped, and then curled up and lay snoring on the ground. The improbable things inspected him. There was fury in the thought-exchanges. But the icy, factual thought came again. This creature's paws were not adapted to the making of artifacts, such as the building yonder, nor the handling of tools required to make artificial lights. So that they should examine the building.

The tiny, loathesome creatures hobbled painfully toward it. Presently . . .

Men carried them back to the craft in which they had come. The men walked with the curious gait of sleepwalkers. And when the men had gone away again the craft that had landed in the forest was filled with rejoicing. Silent rejoicing. Soundless glee. Glee which rose to the status of rebellion. Mutiny took place, with every member of the crew a mutineer and joyously resolved to remain upon this planet for always.

The icy, factual thought again. No gluttony. Not yet. The intelligent life on this planet was highly-developed. If alarmed, it might be dangerous. But if the whole thing were carefully planned and properly carried out. . . . . .

2

THE guard's flashlight played on Jim Hunt for a bare instant before he let go and fell like a stone into the blackness under the dirigible. He felt a raging triumph even as the ship's huge, elongated form shrank swiftly and was blotted out against the stars. The light had played on him at just the right instant and from just the right angle. The guard would swear that he'd been empty-handed, that he'd jumped to his death from the Security patrol ship *Cinquoin* in the darkness and at fifteen thousand feet, rather than submit to recapture. And that was what Jim Hunt wanted.

But the odds were great that the guard would tell the exact truth. As he fell, he had the seat-pack, to be sure. After breaking out of the prison cab, he'd taken it from the crew's cabin of the ship in a desperate stealthy foray down from the maze of braces and wires and billowing, sluggish balloons within the framework of the monster airship. But he'd allowed himself to be cornered and sighted up near the bow, as if he'd been trying in the ultimate of desperation to find some hiding-place in which to conceal himself against search. With honest testimony, now, that he'd leaped to his death unequipped, it might be that the theft of the seat-pack from the other end of the ship wouldn't be noticed. It might be weeks or months before one seat-pack, emergency, type what-ever-it-was, was missed and finally surveyed as expended or lost in the normal operations of the Security Patrol

Ship *Cinquoin*. And by that time Jim Hunt would either be safely hidden—or it wouldn't matter.

Falling with the mounting velocity of a dropped stone and trying desperately to wriggle into the seat-pack's straps, he grew savagely sure that it wouldn't matter. He fell thirty-two feet the first second, and sixty-four the second, and ninety-six the third and a hundred and twenty-eight the fourth. He had one arm through one of the seat-straps, but no more. At the tenth second, he had dropped two thousand feet and was falling at the rate of a mile every sixteen seconds. At the fifteenth second the wind screamed about him as he hurtled earthward. He found himself grimacing savagely, falling through space like a meteor. The wind of his fall ran up the sleeve of his shirt and burst it. And he fought the wildly vibrating seat-pack which trailed behind him. In a nightmare of perpetual falling and blackness he knotted his hand in the strap he could not adjust and heaved. . . .

There was a violent jerk. The pilot-chute was out and tending to check his fall. Another jerk, more violent. The first descent-chute. Then, at two-second intervals, the four horrible wrenching heaves that were the others. Seat-packs, being designed for emergency use in the most literal possible sense of the term, do not contain one large parachute, but five small ones. They open successively, making five lesser wrenchings at a man's body instead of one overwhelming yank which could snap his neck.

At twenty-five seconds after his drop into sheer blackness from the Security ship, Jim Hunt dangled below a swiftly-descending series of parachutes in the midst of a tangible darkness in which no star shone. He should, he believed, be over solid ground. But the *Cinquoin* might have made a detour for some unguessable reason. He might descend into icy black salt sea, or into a lake or even a pond which would serve as well to drown him as the ocean itself.

There was a faint, faint radiance above him. The *Cinquoin* was playing searchlights below. That was quick work, considering. Had he been able to adjust the seat-pack as quickly as its manufacturers claimed, while falling, his drop would have been checked a long way back. The searchlight beams would have caught him above the cloud-bank which now hid him. Either the ship itself would have followed him to the ground, or members of the Security Police would have jumped, too, delaying the opening of their chutes so they'd reach ground before him. Then he'd have been lost.

The radiance, dim at best, grew fainter still and died. The officers of the *Cinquoin* would have the honest statement of the guard that he'd simply jumped. The seat-pack had been hidden behind his body, and he was considered rebellious enough and desperate enough to have committed suicide rather than live the rest of his life in Security Custody. There was no sign of a chute beneath the ship. Everything pointed to his death. The odds were—and he neither saw nor heard anything to lessen them—that the ship had simply gone on to its destination, reporting him a suicide.

He dropped through darkness. Presently a sound like gentle surf upon a beach came up from below, but it came from a wide area. It was a wind of some force, beating upon trees. He set his jaws. He had an excellent chance of being killed in this landing. Or of losing his parachute-string when he struck—to be sighted from overhead when a routine patrol-plane search was made for his body. They wouldn't really expect to find it, unless buzzards guided them, but chutes caught in a tree-top would tell them entirely too much.

There was a sudden increase in the sound of wind-tossed branches. He smelled earth and woodland. He felt branches flashing past him in the dark. Something lashed him cruelly, like a cat-o-nine tails. He struck violently in a pine-tree, and rebounded—but he thought he had broken ribs—and fell in a great, arching swoop, and suddenly he was drenched in a monstrous crashing of water all about him. Then abruptly, the parachute-harness no longer tugged at him and he was knee-deep in a pond or stream, and the sound of wind among trees was a booming sound, inextricably mixed with the swishing of many leaves. And it was overhead.

He felt savagely triumphant. Jim Hunt was dead. The Security Police would concede it without question. The future would take care of itself. But somehow he'd show them! The damned fat-heads! Security! Security! That was the watchword now! They said that science had gone too far. There were a dozen fields in which research might turn up instruments so deadly or principles capable of such monstrous applications that all research had to be supervised carefully. So the World Government was formed; really to protect humanity against the consequences of its own intelligence. Men were capable of such brilliance in dealing with the forces of the universe, and such stupidity in dealing with each other, that mankind had to be protected against itself. But unfortunately the World Government confused the hopes of the future with the real menaces to the safety of the present. Jim Hunt had been solemnly adjudged a menace to the security of humanity. He'd been on his way to a Security Custody reservation to spend the rest of his life in confinement. He'd have been gently treated, to be sure, and allowed even tools and the means of research if he chose —under constant, detailed supervision. But he was to be imprisoned for life.

Now though, he waded ashore in the darkness, pulling carefully on his parachute-lines. It took him a long time to get the billowing masses of cloth—some of it wetted—into a bundle that he could carry and ultimately hide. He neither saw nor heard any signs of human life. But he moved cautiously into utterly black forest, carrying the untidy bundle which had been the compact emergency-chute. He forced his way on at random until he realized that he might be moving in a circle.

Then he lay down to wait for dawn. He was not at ease. If there was the least suspicion that he had escaped, rather than plummeted to his death, Security would hunt him from aloft with infra-red scanners that could note the heat of his body from an incredible distance. There were so many things that could be done if his survival was suspected! And of course a man who was dangerous to Security would be hunted much more relentlessly than a mere murderer.

He could not sleep for a long time. Then he tried deliberately to relax. He would need all his strength and cunning presently. He made his taut, tense muscles relax. He made himself comfortable with parachute-silk under him on a bed of soft woods-mold, scraped together by groping fingers. He lay still and relaxed . . . relaxed. . . Presently he knew gratefully that in a little while he would sleep. . . .

Then there were little nibbling thoughts around the edge of his mind. Not his own thoughts. Alien, patient, insinuating thoughts that were not the product of his own brain.

"Nice. . . ." said the thoughts. *"Nice. . . . Everything is nice . . . This is the nicest place in the world. . . . Everyone is happy. . . . . . This is nice. . . . . . ."*

Jim Hunt made a convulsive gesture and sprang to alertness there in the darkness in an unseen forest. His hands clenched. His heart pounded horribly. Sweat poured out all over his body in streams. He hadn't sweated like this even when he jumped from the dirigible in the hope that while falling he'd be able to work himself into the harness of an emergency parachute. His heart hadn't pounded at this tempo when he was about to land, swept at breakneck speed across the surface of a forest he couldn't see.

He was panting, while his whole body turned cold from the sweat that had poured out over it. The forest was still save for the booming sound of the wind overhead. And now that he was aroused and awake and panicky, it was hard to detect the thing that had stirred him so. But he soothed himself by force of will. He waited, and he was just barely able to feel the nibbling, soothing, insinuating ideas.

"*Nice. . . . .*" came the thought, persuasive but very faint. "*This is nice. . . Everything is nice. Everything feels good. Sleep is good. . . . Sleep is nice. . . .*"

A murderous rage surged up in Jim Hunt's whole body. The nibbling thoughts faded abruptly.

He sat grimly with his back against a tree. His eyes burned in the blackness. When dawn broke, his expression was grim and utterly formidable.

3

SOME WHILE after sunrise he found what might be termed a farmhouse—a log cabin, typical of mountain country where erosion kept cleared land poor and even cattle could not be raised with any great profit. It was not large, and there was a sagging porch and wasteful rail fences and poverty-stricken outbuildings. From hiding, Jim Hunt examined it keenly.

It was exquisitely ironic that he should have defied the Security Police, and been sentenced to life Security custody, because of his experimental work on the amplification and transmission of thought. He had dropped out of the sky in a thousand-to-one attempt at escape, and he'd run into those nibbling thoughts the night before— and they were what he'd been sentenced for. Transmitted thought.

Now he understood some of the Security Police testimony. It had been testified that after an official admonishment not to continue a certain line of experiment, he had attempted to carry on his work in secret. They swore that detectors proved that he continued, and that he had associates or confederates with whom he coöperated. And he knew that the testimony about the detectors was untrue, because his work had been done in a cellar lined with quarter-inch plates of high-hysterisis iron. Nothing his apparatus produced could get through that! No detectors could have caught his fields outside that barrier! So when Security Police gave evidence that he'd continued his work in secret, that was true enough. But when they swore that detectors showed his fields and that he had confederates in research, that wasn't true. He'd thought them liars.

Now he understood. Thought-fields weren't directional. He wasn't sure yet how they could spread out and concentrate again at a distance—and be present in between—and still give no indication of their point of origin. But you couldn't locate a transmitter by any sort of direction-finding device. He knew that. And he knew fully that there was danger in the development of the transmission of thought. But he'd felt that there was greater danger in its non-development.

Those small, nibbling, insinuating thoughts were proof that he was right. Somebody else was transmitting thought. Somebody else was using it for the one purpose that Security most feared—the implanting of beliefs and opinions in unsuspecting other persons. And because it was happening, and because Security had condemned him for studying the problem, and because all worth-while research was now driven underground—why —Jim Hunt was filled at once with a murderous rage and a chilly panic. Everything he believed in was endangered. Those small, sneaking thoughts on the very edge of sleep were not thoughts that the average person would recognize as alien, as directed, as not his own. They would seem to be his own thoughts. With skill, any thoughts could be suggested. He could believe this, or believe that, or that such-and-such was the case despite appearances, and all his will and all his intelligence would be applied to the defense or realization of the ideas he believed his own.

Which was dangerous. Which could be fatal. Even the Nazis, thirty years back, had had no such infallible system for the implanting of false ideas. It was that danger which had made the Security Laws forbid all experiment with amplified thought-transmission.*

*The law read: "An Act to amend an act . . . to amend an act entitled, 'An Act to Regulate and License Study and Research and Various Sciences' . . . Sec. IV. Part 3, Bar. (c). 'The amplification of the physical factors involved in thought, awareness, perception, aperception, reason, knowledge, memory, or any of the phenomena included in human or animal consciousness is forbidden save in official Security experimental zones and under first-priority supervision. The violation of this provision shall be a first-degree offense against Security and may be punishable by death or such lesser penalty as the court may decree.'"

First-priority supervision required that a proposed experiment be described in minute detail and submitted for approval, and that if it was approved it should be performed by Security scientists only, with the proponent advised of the results only if (a) the official Security scientists considered it safe and/or desirable to perform it, (b) if they found the time to do so, and (c) if they felt like passing on the information gained. Actually, restricting a line of research to first-priority supervision meant simply that no research was done.

Jim Hunt had been sentenced for violation of the law. And it was too late to prevent the danger. Security had detectors which could show up the existence of thought-fields, and their intensity. But Security wouldn't allow experiment to develop thought-transmission, because the practice could be desperately dangerous.

But thought-transmission was a fact. It was being used. And Security had prevented the discovery of ways to control it. In all the world only Jim Hunt knew of this specific gap in the Security system which claimed to protect men against their own abilities. But that gap was enough to wreck all of civilization. It was ironic that the only evidence so far was the intrusion of tiny, nibbling thoughts into the brain of one man on the edge of sleep, and that man a criminal for having learned to recognize it.

Now he lay at the edge of a small clearing and watched a log cabin and the languid movements of the family which inhabited it. In three hours he learned that there were two adults and seven children living there. There was a grown girl and two gangling boys in their teens, and the rest ranged down to a baby whom he hadn't seen, but had heard wailing.

All seemed languid to the point where it was unnatural. All were apathetic, as if they were weak. The children of an age to play sat down on the bare earth outside the cabin and fumbled with clumsy toys or talked. They did not run. One of the adolescent boys sat on the edge of the porch and looked vacantly into space. That was all. Toward noon the man of the family went slowly to a nearby field and hoed in it without energy. He stopped often to rest.

Jim Hunt absorbed every movement and every action that he could see. These folk looked unwell. They looked as if they might be chronic sufferers from hookworm. But the farm, though poor and slovenly enough, at least appeared as if there had been work done on it in the past. Yet it was difficult to believe that this lackadaisical, unenergetic family could earn a living on rocky hillside land.

At noon he felt sure that whatever the decision had

been on the *Cinquoin* as to his fate, and whatever or whoever was responsible for the sly small thoughts he'd picked up, he would be in no danger from this family. They had surely no thought of trying to hunt down a fugitive from a Security ship. They had not the energy. And if the thoughts he'd picked up had not been directed at him, but had been picked up simply because he was in the neighborhood of their focus, they wouldn't know of his existence at all. They surely weren't responsible for those thoughts, and in any case he had not much fear that his own reaction to them had been noted. The transmission of thought is difficult enough. To receive clearly from a chosen, unamplified individual consciousness, with other consciousnesses present, should be impossible. So that the transmitter of those soothing ideas of happiness very probably was unaware of his existence. Still. . . .

He wormed his way back into the wood and brushed himself off carefully. He went through underbrush and trees to where a trail led to the farm. He marched confidently ahead. Presently he came out into the clearing. He cast his eyes about as if seeing it for the first time. He walked toward the house.

The children, sitting in the dirt, turned their heads and stared at him. The adolescent on the edge of the porch raised his eyes and looked at him dumbly. The father of the family, off in a nearby field, stopped and leaned on his hoe.

"Howdy," said Jim Hunt, whose crime had been a desire to push back the boundaries of scientific knowledge. "I'm trampin'. Got any grub for a fella that'll work for it?"

The adolescent boy said listlessly, "Y'll have to ask Paw. That's him out in the field. Right lot o' work to do, though."

Jim turned to look at the man who leaned on his hoe. As he looked, slowly and as if with infinite effort that man straightened from his leaning and came toward the house.

"He's coming now," said Jim. "I'll wait."

He sat on the porch. He regarded the children, who stared at him blankly. He began to feel queer. He looked at the gangling boy, and felt queerer. Presently there were slow footsteps and the grown girl came out on the porch. He looked at her and felt very much queerer still. He felt an odd chilliness at the back of his neck. These people, children and all, had an odd expression which was compounded of equal parts of an unearthly tranquility and a settled exhaustion. The net result was something to chill the blood.

They weren't alarming in themselves, but he thought of the sly, soothing thoughts in the night. But for that experience, Jim might have considered this family merely as unusually pale and sickly-looking. Even now he had no real reason to couple their appearance with the terrifying surmises those nibbling thoughts had roused. Reason, indeed, insisted that there was no connection. But the feeling of connection was there.

The grown girl looked at him. She could have been pretty, had she been less pale and thin. She said listlessly, "How-do, Stranger. My, you look strong!" Then she paused, her eyes abstracted. "We don't see many strangers here. Where' you from?"

"Trampin'," said Jim Hunt, remembering to drop the final g. "Just trampin'. You get kinda hungry, trampin', too. I thought I'd try to earn a meal."

The man from the field came slowly up to the house. His face was seamed and weatherbeaten. He had the craggy features of the mountaineer. He had that queer expression of tranquility overlaying exhaustion, too, but in his face there was also an odd content of bewilderment.

Jim Hunt stood up.

"Howdy," he said. "I stopped by to see if I could do some work for some grub."

The farmer looked at him with lack-lustre eyes. He opened his mouth to speak. Then he turned and raised his eyes skyward. On the same instant Jim Hunt heard, too. It was the queer, whispering roar of a jet-rotor. There was a helicopter somewhere near. Which would be Security Police, looking for Jim Hunt's body or some indication of his escape.

The helicopter drifted into sight above the treetops with the Security symbol painted on its side. It came overhead with a swift, dragon-fly-like movement. It halted. The farmer shaded his eyes and stared up. Jim Hunt looked upward, too, with his hand placed to shade his eyes and conceal his face besides. But he was conscious only of an enormous, despairing calm. He was caught. Worse, they'd never believe—.

"*We are Security Police*," barked a voice aloft, through an amplifying loud-speaker. "*A man jumped from a ship overhead, last night. Have you seen or heard of any strangers around?*"

Jim Hunt waited to be revealed. The sudden completeness of his disaster numbed him. He felt practically no emotion. It was too sudden. But he did notice a strange new tensity in the people about him.

Thoughts came yammering into his head. Agitated, angry, raging thoughts.

"*No . . . No . . . No Strangers . . . Nobody at all . . . No. . . . No. . . .*

The farmer cupped his hands and shouted:

"Ain't seen no strangers. Ain't seen nobody but my own kinfolk for a week!"

The amplified voice from the helicopter said, "*He didn't have a parachute. If you find his body, there's a reward.*"

The helicopter moved on above the treetops. It was gone. There was silence. The farmer lowered his gaze and looked bewilderedly at Jim Hunt.

"Now—why'd I say that?" he asked in a weak irritation. "Why'd I tell 'em there wasn't no strangers around when there was him right here?"

The grown girl said quickly, "You was told, Paw. I was scared you wouldn't ketch it. You was told!"

The farmer shook his head, his forehead creased.

"Maybe . . . maybe," he said helplessly. "Seems to me like I'm goin' crazy sometimes. Things come to me, an' I do 'em, an' afterwards seems like I don't know why—an' then I do. . . ."

Jim Hunt swallowed.

"I know why," he said. "It's like a voice speaking in your mind. Mostly it says, 'Nice . . . this is nice . . . that is nice. . . .' Isn't that so?"

The farmer stared at him.

"How'd you know, Stranger?"

Jim smiled very grimly. He knew that he was deathly pale, from the nearness of his capture by Security. But he rather suspected that there was at least as much danger here, trying to be free, as in the defiance of Security.

"Some people," said Jim, "just take that voice for granted. Some people don't. That's all." Then he said deliberately. "How about me working with you long enough to earn some food to carry along with me—" he tried not to let his voice vary by the fraction of a semitone—"and a pot to cook it in?"

The farmer stared at him again. He had been stirred up and enormously stimulated in some fashion. Now the stimulus was wearing off. He said weakly, "All right . . . You get somethin' to eat an' then come out in the field. Bring a hoe with you. . . But I don't understan'."

He went feebly back to the place where he had been working. The grown girl spoke softly. Jim turned with a start. She was no longer listless. Her eyes were wide and intent. She smiled at him warmly.

"Come in the house, Stranger," she said softly. "We'll give you somethin' to eat an' you can help Paw later." Then she said in an amused, confidential tone, "Paw's funny. The Little Fella don't like Paw much. He'll like you, though. . ." Then she said in an eager voice, "Maybe he'll want you to say here. For good! That'd be nice . . ."

Jim Hunt felt his spine crawling as he went into the house. He wasn't sure, of course. He was in a turmoil of emotion, now, and emotion—particularly rage—tends to block out such things as transmitted thoughts. It was the means he'd used to defend himself the night before. But it seemed to Jim that ideas were trying gently and ever so smoothly to worm their way into his mind. And it seemed to him that something was trying to make him think:

"*Nice. . . . This is nice. . . . It would be terrible to go away from here . . . This is nice . . . It will be good to stay here. . . .*"

A surge of fury swept over him. Someone was trying to control him with the very thing Security had condemned him to life custody for trying to understand. Transmitted thought. But fury was an excellent defense against it . . . . .

4

THOUGHTS in the moonlight. Undulating hills and upward-rearing mountains. Spreads of waving forest underneath the stars, Armies of trees, charging valorously over the hilltops. Here and there small clearings and little log cabins with tiny yellow glows in their windows.

And thoughts in the night. Thoughts of glee and gluttony. Of reckless, rebellious zest. Of uproarious and horrible satisfaction—And a cold and icy thought which raged at the others. The native life on this planet was intelligent. Aroused, it could be dangerous. There was need for planning. What had been done was sound enough, but they did not yet control a fraction of the planet's inhabitants. With their numbers, they could not yet control the whole. They must be cautious! They must be wise!

Thoughts of laughter and defiance. Then soberer, drowsy, satiated agreement. Yes. They must be cautious. But these folk, these "men" were such easy prey! They had no idea that thoughts could be projected. They could not communicate with each other save by speech, and their thoughts were feeble and did not carry. It was inconvenient that even stronger minds could not pick up the feeble thoughts of men—but it was convenient because those stronger minds could communicate freely with each other. And since men were such easy prey . . .

Thoughts of sensuous, infinitely agreeable satiation went through the moonlight. The cold, icy thought came savagely again. Caution! It was necessary to learn more about these men before all would be safe! All men were not like those under control. Some knew more. Much more. They had ground-vehicles and primitive flying craft and they could speak to a great distance by their machines. For that matter, a flying craft had been searching these hills today for a man who had jumped from another flying craft. There was organization among these men. If they cooperated—.

A thought said comfortably that the man who had jumped was known. He was under—. The thought hesitated and then said angrily that he was not yet under control. Not yet. But he would be! He was awake, and he raged when thoughts were sent to him, so the thoughts had not yet sunk into his brain. But he would be controlled! There was a female who would be made to lull him. . . .

In the moonlight the icy thought came sharply. If the man raged when thoughts were sent to him, he might know of the sending of thought! It was important that he be controlled immediately and then be made to tell all that these creatures knew, in the primitive speech they used. It was very important. It was imperative! The safety and the—the thought was gluttony—of all of them might depend on what this man knew! They must learn every detail that men knew of control by thought. . . .

The moonlight was bright and tranquil. The trees waved their branches gently in the night-wind. There were little clearings in the forest, and little houses in them, and there was a village down in a valley. There was a city, too, not many miles away, where many folk slept like the people in the mountain cabins. They were pale and thin and they looked as if they had labored to the very edge of collapse. But the face of each and every one wore an expression of an odd, unearthly tranquility, —especially those who were asleep.

The thoughts in the moonlight dwindled. But suddenly there came a triumphant, strong, clear thought. The man who was a fugitive, who had resisted by fury when thoughts were sent to him—that man no longer resisted. Thoughts sent to him no longer—the concept was indescribable, but it meant that they did not remain unabsorbed. Doubtless the man slept now. When he woke he would be definitely controlled, and then everything the wiser men knew would be available. . . .

5

THE WORLD, of course, was bright and new and shining on its sunlit side, and restful and peaceful and secure where night clothed it. In the countries where the sun shone, men and women worked and children played, and where the stars looked down they slept quietly. But all assured themselves that they were secure. They were perfectly, perfectly safe. The world was made safe by Security, which was an organization of quite the wisest men on earth. They were at once the greatest of scientists and the most able of administrators. They had the welfare of everybody in mind.

They had begun, of course by forbidding anybody to experiment with atom bombs, because the human race could be wiped out by only so many of them. They could make all the earth's atmosphere poisonously radioactive. Then everybody would die. But Security prevented that. And presently it forbade the use of atomic energy as such in any form, because, of course, any generator of atomic power makes radioactivity which may escape into the air. And not long after that, the wise men of Security learned that someone had been experimenting with germs and by accident had created a new and very deadly mutation. It could have been used in biological warfare, but it could have released a new and very deadly plague upon the world. So Security forbade experiments with germs. And still later a physicist discovered the principle of a very tiny generator which developed incredibly high voltages. Beams of deadly radiation became possible. So Security had to protect the world from that.

Security was very wise and very conscientious. It did not stop all scientific advance, of course. Its scientists experimented very carefully, in especially set-up Experimental Zones, with all due care that nothing could happen to endanger the people of Earth. Which meant, naturally, that they did not make any very dangerous experiments. And in time Security took a fatherly interest in public health because new plagues sometimes arise in nature, and it issued directives governing quarantine and medicine in general, and of course travel by individuals because individuals are sometimes disease-carriers. And presently it was inevitable that Security should give advice on education, and arrange that technical knowledge should be restricted to stable personalities. In a complex modern civilization a single paranoiac could cause vast damage if he were technically informed. So presently everybody took psychological tests, and those who received technical educations were strictly licensed by Security. Then libraries were combed and emptied of dangerous facts that lunatics could use to the detriment of mankind. And—.

The people of Earth were very secure, to be sure. They were protected against everything that Security could imagine as happening to them. But they weren't free any longer. And the tragedy was that many of the guiding minds of Security were utterly sincere, though there were self-seekers and politicians merely seeking soft jobs and importance among Security officials. The guiding minds believed devoutly that they served humanity by using their greater knowledge and wisdom to protect human beings from themselves. But somehow, knowing their own motives, they did not see that they had created the most crushing tyranny ever known to men.

But Jim Hunt knew it. Yet he knew that even the tyranny of Security, which essayed to control man's actions, was as nothing beside a tyranny which might control their thoughts. Whatever or whoever could sent transmitted thoughts into a man's brain could control his inmost self. A man does not question the opinions his own brain tells him it believes. His mind could become a robot's mind, believing and remembering only what it was told. His actions could become a robot's actions, motivated only by blind and abject loyalty to his unknown master. But even Jim had no idea of the depths of horror the present situation could hold.

He walked with Sally in the moonlight, along the woods-trail leading to the cabin. She pressed close to him, her hand in his arm. The unearthly tranquility of her features was broken, a little, by a secretive half-smile.

"You're funny, Jim," she said softly.

He'd been abstracted, fumbling in the back of his mind for possible intrusive and alien thoughts.

"How so, Sally?"

"You act funny," she said, smiling at him. "You act like you ain't been told!"

"Told what?" asked Jim. Suddenly he was intent. He remembered what she'd said to her father. That he'd been "told" to say to the Security fliers that there was no stranger anywhere about. "What should I have been told?"

"You know!" she protested. "You're teasin' me!"

He hesitated, reasoning swiftly.

"M-maybe," he said after an instant. "What were you told?"

She smiled up at him.

"You know!"

"About what?" he insisted.

"About—us," said Sally. "What we're goin' to do, you an' me. About you stayin' at the cabin for always, an' us—us—."

She smiled confidently up at him. There were prickles at the back of his neck. Then a slow, red fury swept over him. But he said quietly, "Go on!"

"Us—gettin' married," said Sally softly. "I know it was the Little Fella tellin' me I loved you. Oh, sure! But I'd ha' done it anyway! An' when he told me we were goin' to get married I was—awful glad. Were you?"

Jim Hunt stood still. The girl's face was radiant—but so terribly pale and tired! It was unspeakably pathetic. But this was a chance to learn what the victims of those nibbling thoughts could tell.

"Listen, Sally," said Jim, and despite himself some grimness crept into his voice, "when did the—Little Fella tell you all this?"

"While we were eatin' supper," said Sally, still smiling. "Didn't you notice?"

He shook his head, cold all over. "Little Fella" meant something—the source of the whispered thoughts. But no previous guess of his at a transmitter of thought could possibly have earned such a nickname. He had not imagined fondness for the source of the whisperings, though of course fondness could be created by suggestion like anything else. But the use of a diminutive; the complete submission implied in her rejoicing that she was "told" that she was going to marry him; the whole atmosphere of unquestioning acceptance of the control of her life and that of everybody else—these things did not add up.

"I—guess I'm dumb, Sally," he said slowly. "I didn't know about it. I wasn't—I haven't been told yet."

She did not flush. It looked as if she didn't have blood enough in her to flush. But she looked ashamed. Then she said softly,

"But he'll tell you! If he told me, he'll tell you, too! I hope you'll be glad, Jim!"

Jim said bluntly, very cold and raging for the girl before him;

"I came from a long way off, Sally. What is a Little Fella? I've never seen one. I don't know—exactly—what you mean."

She regarded him blankly.

"You don't know? You ain't—." Then she looked frightened. "I shouldn't ha' said anything! I cain't talk about him excep'—"

She caught her breath in terror. Jim put his hand on her shoulder.

"He can't hear what you said!"

"But—but if he wants I should tell him, I—I got to!" She trembled. But it was not quite fear in the normal sense. She was terrified by the discovery that she had done something she should not have done. She was afraid of the fact, not of its consequences. "But—but—oh, sure!" she said presently, self-reassured. "You'll know all about it presently! He'll tell you, an' he'll tell you to love me, if you don't, an' we'll get married an' stay right here for always. . . ."

She was comforted. Jim forced himself to ruthlessness. He asked questions. The answers came. Sally had been told to love him. So she did. Of course! One always did what the Little Fella told one to do. . . . Yes . . . The idea came into one's mind that it would please the Little Fella, and one did it . . .Yes. Of course! How could anybody not do what the Little Fella wanted? How could anybody want to do what he didn't want? The Little Fella was—was—.

There she stopped. There was a mental block that kept her from saying more. No questions, however indirect or shrewd, would bring out anything else. But he persisted.

Presently she said in a choked voice, "He—he tol' me we was goin' to be m-married an'—an' so I was to be awful nice t' you. . . ."

She buried her face in her hands. Abysmal shame overwhelmed her. She sobbed. And Jim, standing beside her in her humiliation, knew that whatever bond kept her subject had been broken. For a little while she could see clearly. But still she could not speak of what she was forbidden to speak. . . .

Presently Jim soothed her as well as he could. He held her comfortingly close and told her gently that he'd only been curious. He didn't know anything about the Little Fella. It was all new to him. But she hadn't done anything wrong. Not in talking to him, because the Little Fella hadn't warned her. And of course when he, Jim, learned about the Little Fella and how people must do what he said, and of course when the Little Fella told him about their getting married. . . .

Her tears dried, somehow. She grew radiant again and somehow maternal. They walked together back toward the farmhouse. Then, when it loomed dark before them with only a single tiny glimmer of light in one window, she whispered, "J-Jim, when we—get inside, you—you kiss me. So's the Little Fella'll hear an' think we' been—kissin' outside. . . ."

Her hand trembled on his arm. He nodded.

He did kiss her, in the dark main room of the cabin,

with no illumination save the dying coals of the fireplace. She gasped, "G-goodnight, Jim . . ."

Then Jim was left alone. And a murderous fury filled him. He had learned much, but not enough. He had not yet had time to sort out what he had learned, but he knew savagely that he had been right and Security wrong, and the danger Security feared had come true more horribly than any Security official could imagine. But his fury was because of the thin, weary, enslaved folk in this cabin. And for the girl Sally.

But he had been a night and two days without sleep, and his mind would not be clear. Also there was the danger that in his weariness the Little Fella—whatever thing devised in hell a Little Fella might be—might put soothing, convincing thoughts into his mind . . .

He went to the fireplace. There was a great iron pot beside it. At the moment it was empty. He held it in his hands. As cast-iron, its hysterisis-constant should be high. He raised it over his head and carefully let down his guard, fumbling in the back of his mind . . .

"Nice. . . ." said the sly and insinuating and somehow loathesome thought. "*Very nice. . . . Sally is nice. . . . Sally is fun. . . . It will be nice to stay here. . . . Sally—.*"

He lowered the iron pot carefully over his head. The thoughts dimmed. He lay down on the corn-husk mattress spread on the floor for him. For a time he was unwillingly alert. Presently he was calm again. He slipped his head partly out of the iron pot. Thoughts came to him once more.

He listened to them in stark horror. Before they could seize upon him—but his horror itself was a defense—he drew the pot down over his head again.

It was very uncomfortable, but ultimately he managed to sleep. And he woke in the morning with the certain knowledge that his mind had not been tampered with while he slumbered. It was quaint to think that he was able to think clearly and think clearly because he'd imitated the fabled ostrich—by hiding his head. But there was sound reason. He'd insulated his laboratory with quarter-inch plates of high hysterisis iron. Nothing his apparatus produced could go through that! An iron cooking-pot neatly if absurdly duplicated the insulation.

But his feelings were grim indeed. The few thoughts he'd dared listen to made him feel sick with fear for the rest of mankind. But it was humorous to know, from that listening, that the iron pot he'd worn had been not only a protection against the thought-field directed upon him, but had absorbed that field so it seemed that he had no protection.

6

NEXT MORNING it became clear that a change was assumed to have taken place in him. Sally's father looked at him with lack-lustre eyes at breakfast. He said heavily, "You' goin' to town today, Jim. When you come back you take over an' finish hoein' the field we were workin' in yesterday."

For an instant, Jim did not grasp it. Then Sally said softly, "Town's Clearfield, Jim. There's a—courthouse there."

Still Jim did not quite grasp it. Sally's mother said with a trace of wistfulness, "It'd be nice to've had it in church, though . . . I always figured. . . ."

Then it sank home. The ridiculous iron pot had protected him not only from transmitted thoughts, but from giving any sign of having been protected. Whatever or whoever the Little Fella might be, the thoughts that had been "told" to Sally and the rest were now believed to have been implanted in Jim's mind while he slept. He was assumed to have absorbed all needful instructions and commands during his slumber. He was believed to have waked with an entire pattern of behavior in his mind, and which had all the effect of his own decision and desire. This family had been told that he would stay in this cabin. That he would help in the fields. That he would marry Sally,—today. In a town called Clearfield. And Sally's mother accepted unquestioningly the fact that he and Sally were to walk into town and be married, and walk back, and that in the afternoon Jim would work in the fields. . . .

They classed him as one of them now. As subject to the same force that made them pale and worn-out robots.

He went white as he realized. Then Sally said explanatorily to her parents, "Jim's goin' to have to talk to Mr. Hagger. I don't know how long that'll be."

Jim said nothing. His flesh crawled at the narrowness of his escape. If a human being knew what transmitted thought was like, he might repel the thought-field of the Little Fella while he stayed awake. Especially if he raged. A thought-field wasn't a radiation. It was a field of force, a strain in space like an electrostatic field. It could be repelled by another thought-field contained in a man's own skull. But during sleep it couldn't be fought off. It would be absorbed. Its absorption would be evident,—like the removal or neutralization of a static charge. And the iron pot that had stayed over Jim's head during the night had absorbed the thought-field directed upon him.

But it was assumed that thoughts had been implanted in his mind during his sleep. Had it happened, he could never again have fought off a transmitted thought by raging, nor have resisted commands transmitted to him even during the day. And if he'd been unaware of the danger he could have been subjugated even while he was awake. Only full advance warning and the iron pot during the night kept him from being, now, the completely abject slave of whoever transmitted orders by thought-field.

Jim found himself sweating profusely. He was to go into this village of Clearfield, since he was believed to be a robot, now. He was to marry Sally in the belief that it was his own desire. And he was to talk to a Mr. Hagger . . . Maybe—maybe this Mr. Hagger was the operator of the transmitter. If so, he must be killed and the transmitter smashed. . . . .

"You remember, don't you, Jim?" asked Sally.

He hesitated. The food in his mouth was tasteless as ashes. But while they thought he was a robot like themselves they would talk freely. Sally had been indiscreet last night because she hadn't known that he was free. On the way to town she might talk again.

"I—guess so," said Jim slowly. "When you say it, I remember. But—my head don't feel so clear this mornin'. Like I—dreamed a lot last night . . ."

"Paw was like that," said Sally wisely. "Sometimes he's like that now. It takes time for you to get used to the Little Fella tellin' you things." Then she said hopefully. "But you're—kinda glad, ain't you, Jim?"

He mumbled. He continued to sweat.

"What time do we start?"

"Soon's we finish breakfast," said Sally. "I'm glad, Jim!"

He felt sick inside. He was desperately sorry for Sally. But he was also desperately sorry for her family and for the others who were subject to this unthinkable tyranny. And there was the rest of the world, too. He, himself, was a criminal in the eyes of Security, but he had upon himself the responsibility for the security of all mankind against a menace Security knew nothing about. He could not yet guess at any plan behind the use of transmitted thought, but its effect upon those subject to it was not only abject mental slavery. There was a physical effect of terrible weakness and lethargy. Anyone who used such a thing could be nothing less than a monster. No ambition or even insanity could make the crime forgivable.

Sally rose from the table and vanished. She came back dressed in her best. There was almost color in her cheeks as she looked at Jim.

"I'm—I'm ready, Jim," she said softly.

He stood up. He felt that he was white as death, but he remembered that Sally had had him kiss her in this same room last night so that the Little Fella would hear and think that they had been—kissing in the moonlight outside. Which was proof that what went on in this room could be overheard. But also it proved that the thoughts of the slaves were not read by their masters. They were only controlled.

He walked beside Sally to the trail in the woods. Once the trees had closed about them, he said abruptly, "How far to Clearfield, Sally?"

"Six miles, Jim." She was quiet; stilled with a quiet rapture. She said suddenly, "Jim! I—I want you should know. The—the Little Fella told me I loved you, but I—I loved you before! You b'lieve that, don't you?"

He said heavily, "I believe it."

They went on. Sally walked steadily, upheld by an inner exaltation. Jim felt himself a scoundrel, but a scoundrel forced by greater need than his own life or his own happiness, or that of Sally or any other individual. If human beings could be reduced to slavery more complete than ever before in all history, something had to be done about it! He said harshly, "I—told you, Sally, that my head wasn't clear this morning. You can tell me anything now, can't you?"

She looked at him with soft eyes.

"I don't know, Jim. If you—ain't seen the Little Fella yet, I don't guess I can talk about him so much. I'm told not ever to talk about him or what he looks like. Not to nobody."

"But that's what I want to know!" said Jim.

She smiled at him, wisely.

"I got an idea," she said, "that you' goin' to talk to the Little Fella that tells Mr. Hagger things. That's why I got to take you to Mr. Hagger. The Little Fella down in the village."

"My God!" said Jim. His voice cracked suddenly. "There's more than one of them?"

"Oh, lots!" said Sally in surprise. "Most every family round here has a Little Fella that tell 'em what to do!— It ain't any harm to tell you that, is there, Jim? Now— now that our Little Fella tells you things?"

Jim's scalp crawled. He almost staggered in his walk. He had been thinking in terms of an individual working a thought-transmitter. He had been imagining a paranoiac, an egomaniac, a psychopathic individual insanely planning the subjugation of the world to his mad will. The horrible part was that it might be done. But this. . . .

He felt weak, suddenly. He said, "Let's—let's sit down a minute, Sally. I feel queer . . ."

She was all solicitude. She took his arm.

"Here's a tree-trunk, Jim. Set down a while. It—takes you that way."

She watched him anxiously. Then she sat down beside him and took his hand in hers. She said regretfully, "The —Little Fella is greedy. . . . It's too bad, Jim . . . The first time you go up to him, specially, it seems like you'll never be able to go down that ladder again. . . . I fainted! But you're so strong, Jim! You'll be all right . . ." Then she said in a startled fashion, "But—Jim! You said you hadn't never seen him!"

A terrible and quite preposterous suspicion was growing in Jim's mind. With it, horror so great that it amounted to panic.

"He's—he's not a human being!" he said, almost shrilly.

His expression called for solicitude again. Sally forgot her bewilderment. She soothed him, smiling anxiously.

"Of course not, Jim! He's cute! So tiny an' so cute. . . . He's the cutest li'l thing. . . ."

He stared at her. But the monstrousness of it was too great even for emotion. When he spoke, his voice was precariously steady. At a wrong intonation he felt that he would go mad.

"This—Little Fella . . . Where'd he come from?— When?"

She said soothingly, " 'Bout a month ago, Jim, we were settin' on our porch 'round sundown when a half-dozen of our neighbors come out of the road to our house. Some of 'em come from a long ways off. They were carryin' things that we couldn't see, at first. They come up an' one of 'em says, 'We brought you somethin' you're goin' to be right happy to have.' An' all of a sudden we knew we were glad. Awful glad! We said we was awful, awful glad to have what they was bringin' us."

Jim made a strangled noise. He could not look at her.

"There was six of the Little Fellas, Jim! The neighbors was carryin' them! An' they was so cute! We knew, right away, that we had to have a Little Fella to live with us an' tell us what to do!" Sally smiled reminiscently. "The folks stayed around about an hour, an' we got gladder an' gladder an' gladder, an' then they went away again, carryin' all the Little Fellas but the one that stayed with us. An' we fixed him up a li'l nest in the attic right nex' to the chimney so's he'd be nice an' warm . . . An' he's been with us ever since, an' we' been glad every minute!"

Jim said thickly, "But he's greedy—."

"Yeah. . . . Awful greedy. But cute, Jim! So cute. . . ." Her finger strayed inside the collar of her dress. She fumbled delicately with the skin. There were tiny scars there. Very tiny scars. One was not quite healed. "Y'don't mind, Jim, he's so cute. . . ."

Jim saw. And he was filled with horror and an all-encompassing rage which was so terrible that for a moment he almost ceased to be human himself. It showed on his face. Sally looked at his expression and shrank away.

"Jim! Are you—mad with me?"

"No!" said Jim thickly. "Not with you! But I'm going to kill that Little Fella! I'm going to kill all the Little Fellas!

I'm going to let the world know what they are and what they do, and they'll be exterminated so terribly—"

"Jim!" She stood up, crying out fiercely. "You cain't talk that way about the Little Fellas! I—I love you, Jim, but you cain't talk about killin' the Little Fellas! They—they —" Then she said in a new, frightened, panicky voice," I— I got to tell him, Jim! I—got to tell the Little Fella what you said! I—cain't help myself. . . . I—cain't—"

Suddenly she turned and ran from him. And as she ran she sobbed terribly. He started up.

But cold reason told him that he could do nothing. Short of kidnapping her and holding her prisoner, he could not do anything at all. Because wherever he might take her, she would still be subject to the Things she called Little Fellas. He knew now they were not human, and he had a blood-chilling suspicion of what they might be. But she should come to no greater harm now than before. The urgent thing, of greater importance than anything else on earth, was somehow to get these facts known to the rest of humanity. Even Security—.

And if he was to get the news away, he must carry it. And when Sally sobbingly reported what she could not help telling, he would be in danger more deadly and more imminent than ever before. Since the Little Fella could transmit thought to humans, once they were subject to him, it was more than likely that he could transmit thought even more completely to his own kind. And that would mean—.

Jim dived into the wood, trying at one and the same time to remember every trick of woodcraft he had learned as a small boy when such things seemed important, and to maintain a fierce, seething, deliberate rage for protection against what might be an irresistible concentration of transmitted thought upon him. Six Little Fellas had subjugated Sally's family while they were awake. Only one had so far worked on him. But there must be many more than six . . . If all combined their power, one man's mere fury might be hopelessly not enough. . . .

7

FLIGHT became a release for all his panic, and he ran like a madman through the trees. He fled crazily until an unseen obstacle caught him across the middle and threw him to the ground. He gasped in fear, and then realized that a single strand of wire had been stapled from tree to tree to form the rudest possible enclosure of a boundary-line. He had run into it full-tilt.

Panic came back. When Sally got home and told the Little Fella, if all the Little Fellas knew and concentrated upon him a concentrated intensity of thought-field, he would stop in his tracks. He would suddenly feel very, very glad that he was going to be subject to the Little Fellas. He would be inordinately happy about it. And Sally might reach home at any instant.

He put his hand on the wire to vault it. Then he realized. He began to work with maniacal haste. He found the nearest stapled place of the wire. He twisted it frantically back and forth and back and forth until it broke. It seemed ages before he had a loose end in his hand. But instantly thereafter he was coiling it feverishly as he moved toward the next point of stapling. His hands shook. He panted in an ecstasy of terror,—not only for himself but for other humans yet unaware. He wound the wire in a close flat spiral, working with more desperate haste than any man in all the world had ever worked before.

He had the spiral big enough. Fifteen—twenty yards

of wire were coiled into an untidy disk some twelve inches across. Then came a soundless thought in his mind.

"Not nice. . . . Not nice to hate the Little Fellas . . . Little Fellas are nice . . . It is not nice to judge them. . . . It is wrong to think of hating them without seeing one to know what he is like. . . ."

Jim Hunt sobbed. This was no tentative, insinuating thought that would creep unnoticed into a man's brain and twist and warp his judgment while he knew of nothing going wrong. This could not be thrust away. This could not be shut out, though he fought it desperately. He tried to continue to make his disk of iron wire. He stumbled.

The thoughts were suddenly stronger. Much stronger.

"The right thing is to see a Little Fella. . . . Yes. . . . Of course . . . It will be wise and nice and good to see a Little Fella . . ."

Then, suddenly, the thoughts were overwhelming

" . . . IT WILL BE TERRIBLE TO WAIT. . . . IT IS IMPOSSIBLE TO WAIT . . . A LITTLE FELLA MUST BE SEEN AT ONCE . . . NOW . . . IT IS URGENT. . . ."

These thoughts were the forefront of his consciousness. He could not think of anything else. They were his thoughts. They were his only thoughts. They were all his mind contained. . . .

He tripped and fell. A sharp branch stabbed his cheek dangerously close to his eye. The pain drove out everything else for the fraction of an instant. And in that morsel of time pure panic returned to him and he clapped the flat plate of wire over his head and pulled it down, stretching it until it covered even his ears. . . .

He stood still, trembling. He had made a disk-shaped spiral of iron wire, and when he pulled it down over his head it stretched into a sort of bird-cage. It was a ridiculous sort of cap. But iron absorbed the thought-field. It weakened it enormously. He could still feel the nagging, compelling thoughts. They hovered about him, trying to take over his brain. But they were only whispers now.

*"Little Fellas are friendly. . . . Little Fellas are nice. . . .
It will be good to see a Little Fella and ask him to explain . . ."*

Jim Hunt vomited quietly. Then he set to work to free
himself from the yet unbroken end of the wire, of which
only one end had been coiled into this eccentric headgear.

When he'd broken the wire once more, he fastened
the cap firmly in place with a strand of wire under his
chin. Then he broke the fence and began to make a second cap. A much more complete one, containing many
more turns of wire and much more closely spaced in many
more turns.

He made the exchange with great caution and desperate haste . . . But the Little Fellas couldn't read his
thoughts. They couldn't know what he was doing. They
lay quietly, greedily, in nests which human beings had
made for them. They thought, and their thoughts went
out and focused, and they waited placidly for the person
to whom they were directed to obey . . .

This second cap shut out the thoughts completely.
They were no longer even whispers. So, very composedly,
Jim made two more. One of the extras he would put on
Sally's head. One he would force on her father who would
not have the physical strength to resist, no matter what
commands the Little Fella gave him. And once his mind
was freed of control by the iron cap, he could be made
to understand, and he and Jim would go and kill the
Thing which lay in a soft nest up in the attic by the
chimney. And then they would equip other men with
caps of wire and—.

It seemed very simple and very sure. A gratified,
deadly vengefulness rose in Jim. Things—mere Things!—
from some unknown hell would take over human beings as
domestic animals, would they? They'd tell humans what
to do? They'd tell them when to love and when to hate?
They'd mate them as cattle are mated? They'd—they'd—.

Jim Hunt ground his teeth and cursed the Thing he

had not yet seen. Their method was clear now. A certain number of them could join to overwhelm the minds of human beings. Once overwhelmed and once conditioned by irresistible powerful suggestion, a human could never defend himself again. One Thing could then control many humans. Perhaps dozens. Maybe hundred. Now the Things controlled this tumbled, mountainous country. Their expansion was secret and piecemeal and irresistible. They had subjugated a countryside and a village, certainly. There was no reason why they should not control a city. A nation. A world! And all without violence, and all without purpose other than that the Things should lie soft and warm and have human beings serve them and be the food of which they were so greedy. . . .

Pure human vanity was outraged at the bare idea that mankind could be subdued to be the cattle, the livestock only, of non-human creatures.

So that Jim was filled with blazing wrath when he set out to put into action the plan which seemed so sure. But it had taken a long time to make the second cap, and the two extra ones. He'd made them very carefully so that not even a whisper of outside thought could penetrate to control a mind whose normal defenses—if any—had been destroyed. He had left the farm in the early morning. He started back two hours before sunset.

He did not try to retrace his steps exactly. He essayed to go back to Sally's home in a direct line. Perhaps two miles from it, he heard the creaking of a farm-wagon. He stopped short. He had almost blundered out upon a hill-country road which seemed filled with country-people.

But there were only men. Most were visibly armed with shotguns or rifles. They were spread out in a long, irregular procession. Most looked pale and thin and sickly. Some few seemed stronger. All wore expressions of unearthly tranquility, save when they spoke. Then they seemed to rage. Jim heard voices.

" . . . Scoundrel!" said a voice bitterly. "Come outa the

woods an' said he was hungry, an' they fed 'im, an' bedded 'im, an' he courted Sally. . . "

Another voice, angrily;

"Even the Little Fella didn't know—"

Other voices said "Hush!" and there was a pause.

"But, by Gawd!" rumbled the first voice furiously, "When him an' Sally started for town to git married, an' he—"

Somebody came spurring back from the front of the line. There were forty or fifty men. There was one wagon. There were half a dozen horses. There were many guns.

"Keep y'eyes open!" commanded the man on horseback. "Maybe he don't know he's been found out yet. He's brash enough to show himself, thinkin' we don't know yet what he done. Try an' ketch him alive if y'can, but don't take no chances on him gettin' away!"

Jim Hunt's eyes flared, ten yards away in the thick underbrush. The sound of his movements had not been heard only because these people made too much noise themselves.

A voice asked harshly;

"She's sure 'nough dead?"

The man on horseback snapped;

"What're we takin' the wagon for? Buryin' tomorrow down to Clearfield! She got back to the house an' told 'em what the fella done, an' she died. He kilt her. He prob'ly don't know we know it yet. He don't know how we git told things. Keep y'eyes open!"

The grumbling, trudging, small-sized mob moved on along the road. Presently it would reach the trail that led up to the farm of Sally's family. It would turn aside there.

Jim remained very still, except that he trembled a little with an icy passion.

He was clear-headed enough though. He knew—now, —the mistakes he had made. The idea that thought-transmission could be accomplished only by human beings had died hard. When Sally'd told him that the Little Fella was something else than human; something that was carried; something that stayed in a soft warm nest; something that was greedy of the life that flowed in human veins—even then Jim had not really grasped the fact. Without thinking it out specifically, he'd assumed that Sally wouldn't be punished for something she could not help. That when she fled back to her home and gasped heartbrokenly that Jim, whom she loved, had threatened to kill the Little Fellas, that her loyalty to that Little Fella would move him at least to mercy in return.

It wasn't so. Sally was dead. And Jim knew quite surely how she'd died. All the family was weak and exhausted and drained of all energy, and she'd said the Little Fella was greedy. If Sally had failed to carry out his commands, what would be more likely than that he'd indulged his greed without restraint?

There is a limit to the capacity of a human being for rage and grief and hatred. Jim had reached that limit. He was numbed. To all intents, Jim Hunt was wholly calm. He could think quite sanely of quite indifferent things. But somehow he did not happen to think of anything but ways to kill, and kill, and kill the Things he had not even seen.

8

HE LAY in hiding next morning and watched Sally's family leave the cabin for Clearfield. They moved very silently, like ghosts. Sally's father and mother, and her two gangling brothers, and the younger children. Sally's mother carried the baby. They filed away into the woods-trail that would lead down to the highway. They looked pale and weak and sickly. It seemed improbable that they could walk the six miles to Clearfield. But possibly a wagon would have been sent up for them. The armed mob that had come up here before was proof that human beings had not ceased to be human, even under the control of the Things. They had emotions of indignation, and surely they would feel compassion and pity, too. Unless they were told not to.

But there was reason for public tumult to be encouraged among humans. The Things, so far, were all-powerful only within their own quite secret domain. Outside, Jim had heard no hint of any strangeness in this part of the world. Security, too, with vastly more information of every sort, could have had no inkling of the enslavement of human beings to non-human Little Fellas. The merest breath of such a suspicion would have had this place swarming with agents of Security. Some would doubtless have been overwhelmed and enslaved by the Little Fellas. But surely some uneasiness would have gone undispelled. The least hint of experiment with atomic energy or bacteriological mutation—X-ray apparatus which could produce mutations was now used only in the presence of a Security representative—invariably led to investigation so exhaustive that all the world dreaded it. And thought-transmission would surely lead to action, if Security got a hint of it. Jim had reason to know that!

So there was reason to have a public excuse for any action which might become known outside the Things' dominion. A wanton and brutal crime resulting in the death of Sally had been invented and was firmly believed in. If Jim were caught, it was even possible that all his questioning would follow all the forms of law. But behind it would be the Little Fellas.

He watched the funeral party of Sally's family file into the woods and go away. Sympathy would go out to them, and fury would rise, and the folk who attended Sally's funeral would turn to and hunt Jim down with a vengeful industry. They had a perfectly adequate motive in the tale they believed of the death of Sally. And nothing would happen to put the rest of the world on guard. Only—Jim had other ideas.

The party of mourners vanished. The world grew silent and still. There still were sounds, of course. The shrilling of insects and the cries of birds, and at long, irregular intervals the plaintive whistle of a bob-white quail. There was bright, warm sunshine. But the tree-branches stirred hardly at all, and the chickens in the farmhouse yard pecked languidly, and the pigs in the pig-pen rooted and grunted without real energy.

Jim watched. And watched. And watched. He was very calm. He knew what he needed to do. It would be infinitely simple, the essential part of it, but he took no chances.

Mostly he watched the trail of smoke from the farmhouse chimney. The whole family had left. Jim had counted them. That should have left the house empty save for the Little Fella. But Jim had his doubts.

He was right to disbelieve. Half an hour after the disappearance of the family along the trail, the thin and steady line of ascending smoke was disturbed. The smoke thickened. Someone had put a log in the fireplace inside.

Half an hour later, a man came out. He carried a rifle. He chopped wood. While Jim was at large and inexplicably immune to the commands of the Little Fella, there must be a guard. Over every Little Fella. This man chopped a little and rested, and chopped a little more and rested. He went slowly back to the house with wood. He came out again and got his rifle. He went wearily into the house again.

Jim moved forward. He'd had plenty of time in which to spy out the land. There was a little rise which would hide him, if he crawled, until he could get the barn between himself and the house. He reached the barn. He was taking a desperate chance, but surely the scene of a supposed crime would be the last place where either the Little Fellas or the humans of this neighborhood would expect him to appear. People and Things alike would expect him to try flight at the top of his speed, to get as far as possible from this place.

Presently he wormed his way out of the bottom half of a door at the far end of the barn. He was behind the chicken-house. It was old and tumbledown. He found a wide plank, partly rotten at the bottom, which could be pulled away. He went inside without showing himself to the house.

There was no alarm. A beady-eyed, abstracted hen sat on a nest. There were other laying-nests about. He crept to the door. Presently a hen entered. He caught her in a sudden snatch. A single squawk and she was still. Minutes later, another hen. A third hen got off a nest and essayed to cluck triumphantly. He caught her.

He was ready. A strip torn from his shirt tied one foot of each hen to one leg of each of the others. He put the three fowl down and crouched inside the door, watching the house through a crack.

The hens squawked. They tried to walk and could not. They scolded each other furiously. They waxed hysterical. They created a sustained, outrageous din, fluttering crazily this way and that as first one and then another succeeded momentarily in imposing her hen-mindedness on the others. It sounded exactly as if some small animal had gotten into the chicken-house and was wreaking havoc among the hens.

It was such a noise as no farm-bred man could hear without investigating. After minutes, a man came slowly out from the house. He carried a rifle, and he walked exhaustedly. He was pale and thin and he wore—Jim saw—an expression of unearthly tranquility. But he came out to see what was scaring the hens.

He pushed open the henhouse door and stepped in. Perhaps he expected to see the darting brown body of a fox go fleeing for the hole by which it had entered.

He found oblivion. Jim swung ruthlessly with a broken

hoe-handle he'd picked up in the barn. The pale, thin man collapsed. When he came to, he was trussed up like a turkey. And there was a queerly uncomfortable cap made out of wire upon his head. Jim had his rifle.

"Listen," said Jim quietly. "With that cap on your head, the Little Fella can't tell you anything. Notice?"

The man gaped, looking at the muzzle of his own gun held unwaveringly at his head.

"Who else is in the house?" asked Jim as quietly as before. His tone wasn't consciously menacing, but actually it was much more frightening than any attempt at threat could have been.

"One man," gasped his captive. "He's—"

"You're going to call him," said Jim gently. "I won't kill him or you, if you do as I say. But you're going to do it! The Little Fella can't stop me. He can't make me do anything. But I can make you do anything, because I'll kill you if you don't."

His face was stone and his eyes were hard as granite. The bound man cried out hoarsely.

"Again," said Jim softly.

The other man came out, puffing. As he entered the chicken-house, Jim hit him savagely. Presently he came to, bound like his companion and with another wire cap on his head.

"These caps," said Jim somberly, "are for your own good. So you won't hear anything the Little Fella tries to tell you. Believe me, you should be grateful to me for that!" He paused and added softly, "I'm the man who came out of the woods and asked Sally's father to feed me. I didn't kill Sally. The Little Fella did that. Being greedy! You won't want to have the Little Fella telling you things for a while. . . ."

He walked openly toward the house, carrying the first man's rifle. Two guards would be plenty for the Little Fellas, and more than two would have showed themselves somehow, in the hour or more he'd watched from the edge of the clearing.

His calculation was right. The house was empty. He went casually inside and helped himself to what food was ready-cooked. He made a search, and found a writing-tablet and pencils. He hunted further, and found faded envelopes. One was a ready stamped envelope. He put them in his pocket. Overhead, in the attic, there was a soft nest close by the chimney. In it there was a small, greedy Thing which had killed Sally, and was one of other Things which were not human and yet dared to subjugate man as domestic animals, for service and use and—food.

Jim did not hurry. He even looked for extra shells for the rifle in the coats of his two prisoners, flung aside within the house. Then he went composedly to the fireplace and took coals and brands from it. He spread them carefully about the building. Some places caught fire readily. Others were not easy to set alight. Clothes and blankets helped though to spread the fire. And the place filled with such a volume of acrid smoke that he was coughing when he went outside.

He waited. Flames rose. They crackled. They purred. Then they roared. Once, Jim shifted the queer cap of iron wire on his head. Very slightly, and very cautiously.

He smiled, with burning eyes. He stood outside a window and looked in. There was not so much smoke inside the house now, but flames were everywhere. The heat was almost unbearable but he stared in hungrily. In the ceiling of the main room there was a little hatch with a ladder going up the sidewall to it. Sally had fainted once, after coming down that ladder. The Little Fella had been very greedy. . . .

Then he saw the Little Fella. He had not seen it teetering in frantic indecision at the edge of the hatchway. He had not even seen it trying dreadfully to use its almost useless limbs to climb down the ladder.

What he did see was a roundish, pinkish, hairless ball, nearly without features, which fell out of the smoke-cloud at the ceiling and plopped on the floor. It bounced

once and then lay quivering. Then it struggled desperately up and it was encircled by flames. It scuttled horribly
here and there, screaming soundlessly. Every way of exit
was barred by flames. It retreated, shaking, shriveling,
flinging itself crazily about.

Jim watched.

He felt no faintest impulse to mercy, but he was not
ill-pleased when a partition fell. Incandescent joists and
burning embers covered the place where the Thing had
stood at bay amidst the fire. And it seemed to Jim that
the fallen stuff quivered a little as if something moved
convulsively beneath it, and he imagined that even
through the protection of his iron-wire cap there came a
sensation like a noiseless, long-continued shriek.

But it ended.

Jim Hunt went composedly away in the hills. He had
a gun and some ammunition. He had food. Rather more
important in his own eyes, though, was the fact that he
had tablet-paper and a soiled stamped envelope and a
pencil. A letter to Security, dropped in a rural mailbox,
could be made demonstrably convincing that he, Jim
Hunt, had survived a fifteen-thousand-foot drop and was
hidden somewhere in these hills. And he could explain
that the people of this area were thin and anaemic and
bloodless, and that the cause would be found to be
thought-transmitters hidden in the attics of their homes.
But those transmitters could be nullified by iron-wire
caps for Security agents.

Again the defeat of the Things who enslaved humans
and fed upon them seemed very simple and quite easy
and very sure.

It wasn't.

9

THE THOUGHTS which raced through the bright sunshine were shaken and raging and terrified. A completely unparalleled thing had happened. One of those who sent thoughts flickering about the hills had been killed. Forcibly, violently, horribly killed. Such a thing had not happened before in a thousand years! Panic filled the thoughts of the survivors. Each one had shared the screaming terror of their fellow as he realized that none of his subject animals—on this planet called men—would come to carry him to safety even at the cost of their own lives. Each one had felt the unprecedented hysteria of helplessness as their comrade shrieked his terror. Each had partaken of his crazy indecision as he looked down into the room which was a sea of flames below him. And each had felt what he felt when he tried, squealing, to climb down that ladder on quite insufficient limbs, to fall instead and bounce sickeningly, and know pain such as every member of their race had been protected from for millenia. And when the flames licked him, and when his hide shriveled and scorched, and when incandescent embers fell upon him, why—such a thing had never happened before! The Things in other soft warm nests, here and there in the mountains, felt their own hairless hides turn crisp and shrivel, and knew all the torment that Thing had known. They could shut out each other's ordinary thoughts, but not the silent pain-mad shrieks of the dying creature.

So that now it was over, the thoughts that raced through the bright sunshine were raging and terrified. The Things had experienced torture. They had experienced defiance. They had suffered agony and known defeat. Some seemed frightened into incoherence. Some seemed temporarily mad. And all had lost the zestful complacency and the placid absorption in their gluttony which had been the portion of their race for ages. Some even clamored for a return to their former home in the craft which had brought them here.

But that was plainly impossible. There were very, very, very many more than had landed. All could not crowd into the craft which had brought the original colonizers. And of course if men were included in the complement, to work the machines and feed the crew—why—not a fraction of their number could depart. So all fought venomously against any plan for safety from which they as individuals might be excluded.

There were ragings and accusations and counter-accusations. A man—a domestic animal—had been able to defy transmitted thought. A man—a source of food—had brought about the death of one of their number. He was still at large. He was still unsubdued. When a dozen of them concentrated their thoughts upon him, each had felt full assurance that their thoughts were absorbed in his brain. They had been absorbed! But without effect. . . .

There came an icy, cold thought in the sunshine. Perhaps it was not a man who defied them, but a member of another non-human race, from another world still, who roved this planet and was immune to the power of their race. If that were so, he must be destroyed. The life of every one of them depended on it. But they must no longer attempt to overwhelm him with pure thought. Men must be used. They must smother him under their numbers. The lives of men did not matter. Every human under their control must search for this creature. If he could be captured by men, that must be done. And he must be handled very cautiously. He could be forced to reveal what he knew of other races able to travel from world to world. Their own race had once been masters of one planet only, long centuries ago. When a space-ship of another race landed on it, the members of the space-ship's crew were overwhelmed by the thoughts of the Things. But their ancestors had been wise. They had not been—the thought was savage—foolishly gluttonous. They had controlled the newcomers, and the newcomers took them back to their own planet, and now the race which roamed the stars was subject to the race which could transmit its thoughts. Here was a new world for them, with an infinitude of subjects to serve and nourish them. With caution, all would go well. But this single immune must be caught and the degree of danger he represented learned. . . .

The icy thoughts went on convincingly. The other thoughts that raced back and forth changed gradually. Some still raged and some still seemed to gibber inco-herently from the shock of the death of their fellow, and the manner of it. But others concentrated their thoughts upon the men under their control. They commanded a man-hunt.

It was beginning when night fell. It continued through the night. It went on through the forenoon, with weak-ened humans collapsing from the demands upon their strength beyond the normal requirements of their mas-ters.

But near midday there came a triumphant icy thought again. The problem was solved! The fugitive had written a letter and put it in a box to be gathered up and taken where he wished it to go. It was directed to be taken to that entity known as Security. It had been opened by a man under control, according to his orders. And ac-cording to his orders he had communicated it to the thinker of icy thoughts. The fugitive was a man, no dif-ferent from other men. He had experimented with the sending of thoughts and had been condemned to im-prisonment. He had escaped, and understood the subjugation of the people about him. He had tried to send this information to the entity called Security, but it was safely intercepted. Security would not receive it. He was only a man. He was the only man who could endanger them. Because Security had forbidden any other man even to study the means by which all of mankind would be enslaved!

The manhunt must go on. If he were killed it did not matter, now. But—the icy thought was suddenly insanely hateful—if he could be left unsubjugated while he was killed very, very, very slowly, it would be more adequate revenge for his insolence in daring to kill one of Them. . . .

10

MORNING AGAIN. Men on watch at every bridge. Men patrolling every highway. Baying bloodhounds in the hills, trailing a man who had killed a girl whose parents had befriended him—so the story ran—and then when her family left their house to attend her funeral, had robbed that house and wantonly set it on fire to burn to the ground. Fury went over the countryside wherever men repeated the story to each other. The Things made them believe it, of course, but they thought it their own conviction.

Rage filled every human being. Bitter, yammering hate of a man known only as "Jim"—Sally's father told so much—and who was described as thus-and-so in appearance, and who wore a foolish cap made out of iron wire. Maybe he was a lunatic. The cap seemed to indicate it.

Sane men didn't wear caps of iron wire. It was illogical and monstrous and immoral to wear caps made of iron wire. If a man wore a cap made of iron wire, though he were your father or husband or brother, he should be seized at any cost in bloodshed and taken at once to Clearfield. No man should ever wear caps of iron wire. . . .

Throughout all the mountains the conviction spread with the speed of flickering, racing thoughts, that no man should ever wear iron wire anywhere about his head. It was the one illogical item in the consciousness of the folk who searched ragingly for Him. But small round hairless things sent out that thought as persistently as they drove the domestic animals called man upon the quest for Him. They could give commands and impose thoughts at any distance, upon their slaves. But men could not report back to the Things except by human speech.

That was the principal drawback to the search—that and the fact that only a verbal description of Jim was available. No Little Fella knew what Jim looked like, save by the description given by Sally's father and her two gangling brothers, and the other description given by two men who had been left bound with caps of iron wire upon their heads. Those two men were now dead. They had not protected the Thing that Jim destroyed so terribly. They had not obeyed Its orders. They had allowed themselves to be knocked unconscious and bound and—via the caps—to be made incapable of receiving orders. And there could be no excuse for failure to serve and protect their master. So they were dead, and two Things had greedily indulged their gluttony in bringing about their death.

But all the skill and wisdom of men and Things was directed to the quest for Jim. The Things sent thoughts to guide the search and keep it at fever heat. Men were told to hate him, and they hated. They were told that he was a monster of criminality, and they believed it. They searched and searched with unflagging zeal, though the bodies of many of them were over-thin and weakened by their masters' other demands upon their strength.

Fresh men arrived to join in the search. They came in heavy lumbering busses, which discharged their loads at first in Clearfield. They continued to arrive as the morning wore on to midday. Sometimes one bus-load at a time. Sometimes a fleet of three or four. Human headquarters were set up in the village. Then couriers were needed, and presently motorcyclists roared into the village, wearing police uniforms. All were raging. All were filled with bitter hate. And all were passionately convinced that any man who wore a cap of iron wire upon his head was somehow sub-human, somehow monstrous, somehow an individual to hate with a poisonous loathing.

Jim Hunt watched the arrival of these outside reinforcements for the hunt with, at first, a blank amazement. He began to suspect the truth only when a fleet of six huge interurban busses lumbered down a dirt road on the way to Clearfield, and he saw them from the brushwood beside the highway. Every bus was jammed with men, civilians all. He saw their faces, and he had not seen too many of the Little Fellas' subjects, but he recognized a certain expression worn by every one. It meant that someone listened regularly to a soundless insinuating thought in his own mind, saying, "*Nice. . . . Nice. . . . Everything is nice. . . . Everyone is happy. . . .*" It meant that a look of unearthly tranquility was a sign that its wearer served loathsome pinkish hairless monsters, and was passionately convinced that he did so of his own will.

But busloads of them! Hundreds of them! Maybe more than hundreds. . . . Commanding the service of fleets of busses at short notice. . . . And uniformed motorcyclists who acted as couriers, showing that there were also official police who served the Little Fellas. . . .

Jim found it hard to believe the sum when he added the facts together. They added up to a certainty worse than he had even suspected. Here in the mountains, one could believe that the Little Fellas could seize a whole population without the outside world having the least inkling of the fact. But these hordes of men of all conditions—Jim saw worn, exhausted figures among those to be glimpsed through the bus-windows—meant more than a rural population enslaved. Either a town of middling size was utterly subject to the Things, or at the least a city was in process of being silently and insidiously conquered.

Sally's family had been subjugated instantly neighbors came bringing Things cradled in their arms. The neighbors stayed one hour, and went away again, and a Thing was nestled in a soft warm nest in the attic and Sally and all her family were joyously subject to him in their inmost thoughts. The same thing could be done in a city. A party of friends might readily carry small round Things from one house to another, and one family after another would be seized upon, and each would instantly be very, very glad that there was a Thing in some soft warm nest nearby, who told them that all the world was nice. . nice. . and that they wanted nothing more than to obey him in all things. They would keep the secret of his existence with a desperate loyalty. And they would open their veins to satisfy his gluttony and feel a shivering ecstasy as they made the sacrifice.

Even a guest in such a household might feel a nibbling glow of contentment ,and a desire to return often to a place where such a feeling of joy was to be found. Sooner or later he would find himself irresistibly asleep—a voice in his own mind would whisper "*nice. . . it is nice to doze off. . . just for an instant. . . .*"—and he would sleep and wake up very happy indeed. Permanently happy, provided only that he was allowed to obey the Thing in the soft nest—so cute!—and share the subjection of the others in all things.

Yes. A city could be taken in that way. House by house. Family by family. Neighborhood by neighborhood. And if the Things were wise and understood the civilization of men, they would surely make the leaders of the city their first subjects! The police, naturally. And the doctors too, of course! Perhaps especially the doc-tors, because sometimes a Thing was less than wary and forgot caution in its gluttony. A human might faint, or visibly be white and bloodless and exhausted though wearing a look of unearthly tranquility. The doctors should be enslaved first of all.

Two more busloads of men went by, to join in the search for Jim. It was then four in the afternoon. The Things were reckless in their need to capture him. He had defied them, and they could not subjugate him, and he had killed one of their number. They were mobiliz-ing their slaves in overwhelming numbers to beat the mountainsides for him. He knew their secret. He knew that such things were, and he did not adore them. At any cost he must be destroyed, though it meant the use of a mob numbering thousands, drawn from many miles away, and though it was hardly convincing that the murder of an unknown mountain girl, the burning of her parents' home, would cause much stir except among her neighbors.

Even with the evidence of the busloads of men, it was not easy to accept the implications of their presence. Such an army, mobilized so swiftly, implied a deeper horror and a greater danger than even he had been will-ing to sacrifice himself to defeat. And then came a creepy panic on top of all the rest.

It was ironic. He'd defied Security to carry on research in a forbidden subject. He'd hated Security because it changed an ideal of safety into one of sheer stagnation. He'd rebelled against it because it tried to force an ex-change of security in the place of hope. He'd been one of those who said bitterly that Security tried to make life so safe that everybody would die of boredom. But the terror that beset him now was not less real because it was ironic. He was afraid that Security itself was sub-ject to the Things!

In his letter, he'd said he would contact the patrol-ships when they came to investigate the statements he had made. He would surrender himself to life imprisonment in exchange for the chance to prove a danger Security did not suspect. But now he no longer dared to think of keeping such a bargain.

He turned from the dusty roadside and plunged back into the woods. Far away, he heard the baying of hounds. But it would take much time for them to unravel the confusing trail he'd left. He had a resource, and now was the time to use it.

A hundred yards back, a man lay on the ground. He had been one of those who searched for Jim. He'd been white and exhausted even at the beginning, because the Thing he served was greedy, too. But he'd been commanded to join the search and he'd obeyed. He'd driven himself with ruthless resolution, spurred on by the fury he'd been commanded to feel. He'd gone to the limit of his strength and beyond it, using up every non-existent ounce of energy, stumbling when he could not walk erect, staggering when his muscles would not obey his commanded will. When he'd dropped, it had been because there was no strength left in him. Jim had found him in a coma caused by something far beyond fatigue. The man was apt to die of pure exhaustion, and it had been Jim's intention to carry him to the roadside and leave him in plain view, in the hope that sheer humanity might lead someone to pick him up. Of course, if he were brought back to health he would only return to impassioned loyalty to his gruesome master, but still. . .

Jim, though, could no longer practice humanitarianism. If he was the only living man who suspected the existence of the Things without being subject to them, and if their conquest had spread beyond the mountains as their mustered army showed,—why—his own life had to be preserved until he could give warning.

He did not feel heroic. He felt, rather, a sickening scoundrel. But he stripped the barely-breathing, uncon-

scious man. He donned that man's clothing. He dressed
the limp figure in the garments he had worn and that he
knew would have been described to all who sought him.
He dirtied the other's face and clothes with mud, as if
he'd splashed through swamps and rivers in his flight.
And then he added the final touch.

He put a new cap of iron wire on his substitute's head,
and fastened it with a strand beneath the muddied chin.
He took the other's headgear and put it on his own head.
It hid the cap he still must wear or risk the subjugation
of all of earth. And then, unhappily, he gauged his wait-
ing-time by the sound of dogs baying urgently in the distance, and dared to wait till dusk.

At dusk he went out into plain view on the dusty highway. He carried the limp figure he had hoped to help,
but now would quite possibly destroy, over his shoulder.
He trudged along the highway's dusty length.

He had carried his burden almost a mile when he
heard the soft turbine-purr of a bus behind him. He
turned and waved. He pointed to the cap of iron wire
on his victim's head.

That was enough. The bus stopped. Men dragged the
muddy, unconscious figure within. Jim climbed aboard.
No one asked him questions. Every man stared hatefully
at the prisoner. There was such rage in their eyes that
it seemed a tangible thing. They had been commanded
to hate a man who had murdered a girl and wore a cap
of iron wire on his head. A cap of iron wire! That had
been commanded to be considered a greater crime than
murder! It was loathsome beyond imagination! That kept
every eye upon the feebly breathing prisoner while men
panted hate of him.

When the bus reached Clearfield, Jim got out with the
others. There were only three people who could recognize him if they saw him, though he counted on two
others who now were dead. But in the crowd he went
unnoticed.

He waited. The limp figure went swiftly out of the

bus. It went swiftly to the place appointed for it. It had an iron-wire cap on its head. It wore Jim Hunt's garments. It was unconscious, and could not be questioned. But identification was complete. Just after sundown, the mob was told that the hunt was over.

Then, swiftly and smoothly and very promptly, the mobilization was reversed. Parked busses opened their doors to take on their loads of now-no-longer-raging men. Jim climbed into the first of them and took a place on the farthest-back seat. The bus filled to suffocation. Its turbine purred, and it rolled softly and gingerly over the uneven highway in Clearfield, and lurched cumbersomely over the narrow dirt-road beyond.

Presently it trundled down a ramp to a great trunk highway and picked up to its highest permitted speed. Jim leaned back against the end-wall and pulled his hat down over his eyes. He was very careful, though, not to let his iron-wire cap show.

In half an hour, the bus discharged its passengers in a city street. Early night grayed all the world. The bus's passengers melted away in as many directions as there were men. There had been no talk on the bus. There was none now.

Jim went to a pay-visiphone booth. He put a coin in the slot and said curtly, "Security."

The screen lighted, and he saw the reception-desk, with a uniformed Security Police officer looking uninterestedly at him.

"Business?" said the screen without animation.

"Look!" said Jim. "Here's something I found. I—don't know whether it means anything, but—"

He held out an object of which he had made several specimens, trying to arrive at one that would not be too uncomfortable for his own use. This, like the others, flattened out readily into a spiral disk of wire.

"It looks," said Jim, "like it was meant to be a cap. A sort of cap made out of iron wire—I wondered—"

Then he ceased to wonder. The face of the Security

officer twisted with instant, commanded-reaction loathing. He reached quickly to press a button. . .

Jim got out of the visiphone booth in a hurry. Even
so, he was only a block and a half away when the patrols
flashed into position from every direction and formed a
cordon about all spaces within a block of the booth. Nobody would get out through that cordon without positive
identification and a precise account of why he was at
that particular spot at that particular time. If he wore an
iron-wire cap—

Jim had barely slipped through. He went on hastily,
like everybody else when a Security cordon was thrown
about an area. But he felt deathly sick and much more
lonely than he had believed a man could be.

The Things had control of Security, too. At least here.
If they had chosen to take over its very top levels—
which was surely possible—if they controlled Security
itself, there could be no hope for mankind.

11

SECURITY, of course, had the final and overriding power
among men, and it differed from previous tyrannies only
in degree. The sincere belief of its top men that they
were essential to mankind's continued existence had only
little more reason behind it than the similar beliefs of
previous dictatorships and empires. Men had reached a
stage of technical progress where they could destroy
themselves, and something like Security, to some degree,
was needed. When it was a purely international affair
and hardly operated below a national level, it was prob-

ably an unmixed blessing. It certainly prevented a second atomic war and assuredly kept biological warfare from being tried out full-scale.

Even later it was essentially useful. It wouldn't be wise to allow high-school students to learn the principles of induced atomic detonation. Common table-salt contains a fissionable isotope and adolescents playing with atomic energy could be more destructive than even with fast cars and sport-planes. Also, it was even necessary that cranks and crooks and lunatics should not be able to go into the nearest public library and find out just what a single individual can do in the way of damage with proper information and a minimum of aparatus. When Security managed only these things, even, it was not too bad. But there is a boundary to the safe suppression of knowledge.

Security no longer recognized limits. There is a point where risks have to be taken for progress. When Security extended its authority downward and prohibited all dangerous scientific experiments, its underlings ruled automatically that anything which could be dangerous should be forbidden, and that any experiment whose result was not certain could be dangerous. Interplanetary flight could not be developed because any but one-way guided-missile flights meant a danger of bringing back alien and possibly deadly micro-organisms. Microbiology became merely an art of cataloging observations, because bacteria sometimes mutate under cultivation. Experimental medicine became pure science without application to human life, and physics. All research involving nuclear fission was forbidden and physics came to a frustrated stop. Even electronics was suspect. When Jim Hunt essayed a daring excursion into the physical basis of consciousness, the foreseeable perils of the subject made Security clamp down swiftly and firmly for the safety of mankind.

The official motive for Security decisions could not be

challenged. Its motive was the safety of the race. Nobody outside of Security was allowed to learn enough to be able to challenge its methods. The world as a whole tended to settle down into a comfortable stagnation, with due gratitude to Security for its continued life, and most people placidly confided in the protection they were not allowed to escape.

But this state of things was ideal for the purposes of the Things. Naturally enough, as parasites, they were not especially intelligent. Certainly not, compared to men. They were utterly uncreative. Essentially they were parasitic in exactly the fashion in which lice are parasitic, only with a highly specialized ability to implant desired thoughts into the consciousness of other organisms. That was all. This odd power secured their survival, instead of small size and ability to hide which lice and fleas find so convenient. The Things thrived because they could make other creatures wish to serve them, instead of kill them. They had a very considerable cunning, and certainly they had the ability to learn a great deal about their hosts—or victims. But despite their success they were actually rather stupid.

They had exactly one desire, to be warm and comfortable and fed. That happy estate called for the enslavement of other creatures intelligent enough to provide warmth and comfort and food. Actually, the Things had only one technique and one trick, but the combination was deadly. The technique was the linkage of their thought-transmission power so that several could concentrate on an individual on whom they wished to prey. The trick was the use of slave-brains for contrivance.

When desire to serve the Things became a passion as sincere and unreasoning as patriotism, their victims set joyously about the enslavement of their fellow-men. They schemed for it. They planned for it. They devised far-reaching and beautifully-planned campaigns to bring it about. And they had no qualms, because everyone who was subject to the Things was very, very happy. It showed on their faces. But of course a man in a state of inner exaltation is not so good a workman, and there is a fine edge gone from his perceptions because he is lost in his contentment. Also there are times when he is desperately weak because of the Things' demands upon his strength. So where the Things held sway there was a slight slackening. Civilization seemed to falter just a little, in preparation for a quiet and contented descent into barbarism. But when the service of the Things was the high point in one's life, and they wanted only to be warm and lie soft and feed gluttonously,—why—there was no point in striving for anything more.

But Jim Hunt was not yet reduced to slave's estate. And his freedom was the only thing the Little Fellas had to fear, and about the only hope for yet-free humans to stay that way.

Long after nightfall he still roamed the streets of the city and racked his brains for a possible course of action. At any instant a deadly and desperate search for him might begin again. The unconscious man he'd turned over in Clearfield had been accepted as himself. But if Sally's father looked at him, or a physician were ordered to restore him to consciousness . . . Yes. A doctor-slave would see tiny scars, fresh ones, which would prove that the man in the iron cap had been a duly submissive slave and could not possibly have been Jim. A blood-count would show weakness beyond exhaustion, and its cause. Unless that man was simply murdered out of hand, it was inevitable that he'd be found to be an unwitting imposter.

And when that was found out, of course it would be guessed that Jim himself had turned him over. And that Jim had very quietly mingled with those who then gave up the hunt and had been carried out of danger when the summoned mob returned to its homes. And there was his call to the local Security office. It had seemed a safe trick. Somebody might make such a call in all innocence. But no innocent man would have fled with such speed when the Security officer in the visiphone pressed an emergency-button. Only a man with a bad conscience would have suspected that the button would trace the visiphone call and order a cordon about it instantly.

So Jim should be in as bad a case as ever. If Jim's substitute had been unmasked, the odds were a hundred to one that he was already being hunted in this city. The police-force here was under the Things' control, and there was an infallible way to detect Jim. He wore an iron-wire cap. Already there would be a cordon about the town. No man could leave on any vehicle, ground or air, without removing his hat at least, and probably not without a more detailed examination still. They'd know Jim had to get away quickly and that he'd guess it. So they'd try to trap him.

He couldn't stay in town without taking off his hat. By morning there would be an order that all men had to take off their hats in all public vehicles. In all stores and dwellings and places of business. It was absurdly simple! If it was announced that the homicidal maniac who'd committed a crime of insensate violence and wanton horror in the mountains was now in the city, the entire population would look for him. If it was announced that his mania commanded him to wear a cap of iron wire on his head, even the children would challenge any man who kept his head covered!

So simple! People who were enslaved would seize him in a frenzy of hate. People who weren't would shrink in horror from the iron cap that proclaimed him a lunatic. And if he tried to explain? Small round hairless things, horribly gluttonous and cuddled in soft warm nests, served by humans who were their passionately loyal slaves? No one would believe his story. They'd fear him. Broadcasts and newscasts and published accounts would make him hunted everywhere. Everywhere! Within ten hours there was not a city on the continent where he would be safe or where he would be listened to!

It was airtight. Even Jim's few friends would think him mad. News accounts of the murder he was accused of would take care of that! Simply by the accusation of murder and the necessary wire cap, he had become a psychopath, a deranged criminal, whom absolutely nobody on earth would listen to. Logically, he would even seem to have gone mad as a result of his own experiments and to have proved the wisdom of Security in forbidding them.

In this completely hopeless reasoning, however, Jim had made an advance. Until now he had believed in horrors only when they were proved to exist. But now, abruptly, he thought ahead. For the first time he anticipated future troubles.

". . . . . *is believed to be possibly in this city. Without alarming the public, the police give information that a man seen wearing an iron-wire cap is apt to be a homicidal maniac and likely to commit a murder at any time without provocation. It is suggested—*" Here the newscaster's face wore a reassuring smile, "*that every man in the city go hatless tomorrow, and that all citizens beware of any person who approaches them with his head covered. If you stay away from any man who can be wearing an iron-wire cap, you will be quite safe. . . .*"

It didn't even increase his numbed feeling that absolutely nothing could be done. The only way to convince anybody who wasn't already enslaved, he reflected with surpassing bitterness, would be to show them—.

Then he stopped short, there in the shadowy street with tall dark buildings on every hand. He was unshaven and shabby and in ill-fitting clothes. He had been condemned to life imprisonment, and had escaped, and now he was a hunted animal, and any other human being who saw him tomorrow would scream with terror if he drew near them with his hat on, and scream more horribly still if he took off his hat. . . .

But the despair suddenly left his face. His expression

grew drawn and taut and intense. After a moment he moved on, but his eyes roved now, seeking what he knew he must have.

An hour later he idled down a very narrow street in the oldest and dingiest part of the city. The shops here were cheap and shoddy. Their interiors were dark. There was a vague smell of mustiness from the very buildings.

He'd passed the shop once walking briskly, and again walking with the listless gait of one whose Thing was very greedy. This third time he slipped into the vestibule. He broke the narrowest panel of the shop's plate-glass. There is a trick to doing it without noise, and he used it. In seconds he was inside the shop, ransacking it feverishly.

He went out of the window with a heavy bag in his hands. The bag contained saleable loot—purses, handbags, silk scarves, and the like. It contained a wax display-head, on which mannish hats were set to show how fetchingly they would make a wearer look. And he had a lot of assorted scissors.

An enterprising thief would have realized money on the lot. But Jim carried it three blocks and turned into an alley—this was a very old part of the city, built before the Second World War—and crouched down in an alcove between buildings. He had spotted this place, too. There was a storm-sewer grating there. And he carefully thrust all his loot, piece by piece, into the opening. He thrust the bag through. Then he smashed the waxen head and put every scrap of wax deep down out of sight.

With an obvious looting of the store for marketable goods, the theft of the wax head might not be noticed. He'd shifted the remaining display-heads, too, to hide the fact that one was missing. Absorbed in the loss of merchandise, the proprietor of the shop might not notice for days or weeks that a window-dummy was gone.

And an hour later, his face grayed with whitish dust rubbed off on his hands from a whitewashed wall, Jim

Hunt stumbled into a starting-place for busses. One of the smaller vehicles was just warming up, getting ready to leave on a route which included Clearfield.

Jim stumbled wearily into it. He was the only passenger, so far. He paid his fare. The conductor said shortly, "Hat!"

He pointed to a new sign in the bus's interior: ALL MEN'S HATS MUST BE REMOVED.

Jim numbly took off his hat. He visibly did not wear an iron-wire cap. He looked drawn and gray and exhausted. He went with dragging footsteps to the very back of the bus and sank down in a seat.

A little later the bus rolled out. It had two other passengers, no more. It purred through the city streets. It was stopped once at the edge of town. The driver spoke curtly to a uniformed man who peered within. The uniformed man glanced at the passengers. A fat woman, and a bald-headed man, and Jim seemingly comatose from weariness in the back. One of the bus's lights shone on Jim's uncovered head. The policeman was satisfied. The bus rolled on and out into open country.

Jim continued to look half-dead and wearied. Actually, he felt almost incredulous of his escape. A wig from a fashion-dummy, caught over his iron-wire cap and unskilfully trimmed to blend with his own hair had not seemed promising, but it was the only trick that he could even try. Still, it was not likely that anyone would look for the fugitive who'd been hunted so desperately in the mountain country to head back for that very area when he made a break out of the city.

From his own standpoint, though, he could have no other destination. Anywhere in the world, his unsupported tale would be considered the raving of a lunatic. Now that he'd been accused of murder, even Security would think he'd simply gone mad. Unless the Things controlled Security. There was just one possible action for Jim to take.

He had to kidnap a Thing and get away with it to where free men could be persuaded to examine it and credit the meaning of its existence.

12

WHEN THE BUS let him out on what seemed mere empty country road, some ten miles short of Clearfield, he found it hard to believe. As the bus went purring away into the night, he felt so terrific a let-down that for a moment or two he was as weak as he'd pretended to be. Until the very last second he'd been afraid of some such absurd accident as his wig falling off, or that the bus would suddenly arrive at a place where forewarned men would be waiting to receive him as the object of their search.

But nothing happened. He was alone. Katydids sang in the darkness. Frogs croaked somewhere in the night nearby. A whippoorwill senselessly and monotonously repeated its refrain. There was a soft rustling of tree-branches. Once he saw a moving light, and panic filled him, and it was a firefly.

He stepped across a shallow ditch in the starlight and worked his way into a wood. He blundered through it until he felt open space before him and an iron-wire fence such as seemed to be used here either as boundary-markers or to restrain unusually docile cattle. Here was a clearing. He followed its edge around to the other side, because at the edge the ground would not be ploughed and would show no tracks. He went farther and farther from the highway.

He found himself wading through knee-deep fallen

leaves, gathered in a hollow by some vagary of air-currents. He was very, very tired and numbed in his mind. He lay down and prepared to sleep, and his wire cap shifted on his head. He started wide awake, cold all over. He'd modified the design of his wire cap, of course, so that it stayed more or less firmly on his head without a wire-strand under his chin to hold it on, but it would not be safe to sleep that way! He'd almost gone to sleep without fastening the cap so it couldn't be dislodged while he slumbered.

He fixed it, but the near-lapse frightened him. He lay awake in the darkness, listening to the tiny small sounds of the night. And this shock of fear had an odd effect. It suddenly occurred to him that not only the story he had to tell but all his actions were those of a madman. He had seen one Little Fella, one Thing. It was a preposterous, roundish, pinkish ball that bounced when it fell, and then quivered as flames licked at it. .

But his memory could be a delusion.

He could be insane. He had experimented with thought-amplification, and it was desperately dangerous. Security was quite right there! It was quite possible that in his basement laboratory, with its quarter-inch steel walls, his brain had been affected by the thought-fields he had made. The infinitely delicate organization of his memories and his perceptions could have been disarranged. Neurones could have become distorted in function because they were subjected to the stresses his fumbling apparatus had produced. Perhaps he had committed the crimes of which he was accused! Combined delusions and memory-lapses would account for everything. . .

He had been under a ghastly strain of panic and of horror. He was poisoned with fatigue. He felt an impulse to tear off the iron-wire cap and find out once and for all whether he was mad or not.

Sleep came suddenly, at long last, and then he slept heavily. Only toward morning did he dream. Then he was lecturing lucidly to that eminent person, Doctor Phineas Oberon, the Security Director of Psychological Precautions. Doctor Oberon sat fatly back in his chair and listened with the complacency of the third-rate man in a position of authority.

"It's perfectly simple!" Jim was saying exasperatedly. "Consciousness isn't a radiation. It's a field of force! In effect, a static field! In our brains it governs the degree and distribution of excitation of the neurones! And we simply haven't had the instruments with which to examine such fields in detail, before! I've made 'em! You can check the theory and try 'em out! And there's a generator of the field that can be hooked onto the scanning instrument—the modulator—and make the same field all over again with greater intensity! It's so simple!"

"My dear young man," said Doctor Oberon complacently, in Jim's dream, "your proposal is illegal. Section IV, Part 3, paragraph C of the Security code as amended reads, 'The amplification of the physical factors involved in thought, awareness, perception, aperception, reason, knowledge, memory, or any of the phenomena included in animal or human consciousness is forbidden save in official Security experimental zones and under first-priority supervision.' The violation of that provision is a first-degree offense against Security."

"But dammit," cried Jim shrilly in his dream. "It's got to be done! It's—look! We make electricity in our bodies, but electric eels do it more strongly. We make thought-fields in our brains, and these Things do it more powerfully. But just as we can electrocute an electric eel with a dynamo, despite its power, we can handle the Things—"

"It would be quite illegal," said Doctor Oberon with finality. "And you are disqualified for consideration for experimental work in any case, because of your conviction of a breach of Security—"

"But man!" cried Jim in the impassioned urgency of dreams. "Don't you realize? All that's needed—"

Then he opened his eyes, and he was half-covered with fallen leaves, and it was broad daylight, and birds were singing, and he was very hungry.

He stood up slowly. In his dream he had known exactly what needed to be done to destroy the power of the Things at once, but he couldn't remember it, now that he was awake. He puzzled over it a little. Of course, in dreams we all have marvelously brilliant thoughts, which usually turn out not to be so brilliant when we examine them in daylight. But this had been unusually convincing. It seemed to have been completely logical and completely reasoned out. In the dream he'd known not only why he was urging that something specific be done, but how it would work and what its effects would be. But it was all gone now.

After a moment he shrugged. He was one man against Security, and the Things, and all the slaves of the Things and everybody who believed the perfectly reasonable things that both the Things' slaves and Security had to say. The tale he had to tell was so preposterous that he'd doubted it himself. There was only one way to make anybody even begin to believe it, and that way wouldn't be easy. But he literally couldn't stop. He couldn't surrender. He couldn't make terms. He could blow his head off with the pistol he'd taken from a man he'd first intended to help and then turned over in his own place, or he could find a good deep pond and jump into it. There was no other way to end the hunt for him. But since he was finished anyhow, he might as well play it out.

He searched for a wire fence. It took him a long time to find a single-strand one. He came upon a hog-lot with a low woven fence about it, and took warning from it. He moved more cautiously after that. It was an hour before he found what he wanted—one of those single-wire barriers that formally marked off a boundary in woodland and perhaps served to hold back cattle or horses from wandering. He broke the wire and set to work.

He was hungry, and it annoyed him to be bothered by hunger when his life could be measured in hours, at most. It bothered him, too, that he had to make something out of wire with no tools but his hands, and that he could afford to take no chances at all,—that it must be unqualifiedly right.

He had the job halfway done when he saw a fatal flaw in the design. He had to start all over again. It had been late morning when he began, and noon came and he was irritatingly ravenous, but he forced himself to work with painstaking precision. He could not cut the wire save by repeated bendings until it broke. His hands grew raw. Blisters formed and broke. His fingers bled. He kept on doggedly. When at long last it was finished, with loose ends devised so he could twist them together and fasten it and nothing short of pliers would ever loosen it again, he went to a small stream and drank heavily.

Then he rested, looking rather grimly at his hands. He remembered, too, and used a still spot in the stream for a mirror, to see how convincing his wig might be. It was not too good. He trimmed it a little more and twisted odd strands of the hair under his iron-wire cap for still greater security against its slipping off.

Again he had to wait for dusk. It would make his story less likely, but he did not dare to risk close inspection. There were some factors in his favor, but this was a late hour at which to appear. . . . But he had to wait for dark so his wig wouldn't be looked at too closely.

He retraced his steps to the clearing he'd circled the night before. There was a farmhouse close by the main highway. He watched it for a long time. It was a prosperous farm for mountain country and poor land. The house itself was trim and neat and newly painted, and the barn was large. There was a flower-garden and a small building that could only be a garage. Decidedly this was a prosperous place. If there was a Thing here—and there must be—within half an hour of darkness his fate and probably that of the world would be decided.

The sun sank with an agonizing slowness, but as dusk drew near Jim moved cautiously along the edge of the clearing toward the farm-buildings. There were mountains all about him; great mounds of forest-clad stone, here and there broken by precipices of naked rock. There was a vast, serene dignity in the hills. Men had subdued their lower slopes, to be sure, but the mountains stood aloof from mens' petty doings. Still, their dignity would become scorn should men become subject to loathsome, shapeless, alien Things, who lay soft in warm nests and commanded humans to be their slaves and satisfy their gluttony. . . .

Jim, however, thought of no such abstract ideas. He clung to the object he had made, and felt the smarting of his hands which were caked with dried blood, and he knew a monstrously irritating hunger. When dusk began to fall he risked much to creep out into the orchard and gather a dozen wind-fallen apples. He wolfed them, rotten spots and all.

Then night came, quietly and with a brooding peacefulness. There was the sunset hush. There were all the minute, soothing sounds of ending day. Birds made drowsy noises and chickens cackled as they were fed in the farmyard.

Jim took off his coat and wrapped it with a vast care about the object he had made. It had to be done just so; to give an effect of enormous solicitude, and yet to be uncoverable instantly and used without the fraction of a second's delay.

He began to stumble toward the house with the air of a man at the very limit of his strength. He looked drugged and dazed by weakness and fatigue, and yet blindly obeying an implanted instinct of faithfulness. He seemed to be carrying a heavy object—though the thing he had made was not heavy at all—with all the tender and protective care one would give to a human baby.

13

It was early night. Lantern-light streamed out of an open door in the barn. He stumbled to the light and stood there blinking, with the coat-wrapped bundle cradled tenderly in his arms. He made his face seem to work with exhaustion and his breath to come in gasps.

"Listen!" he panted. "You—you got a Little Fella here? I—got to show him somethin'! I—I—"

The farmer was an oldish man with an expression of vast patience—and of course unearthly peace. He was milking a cow. He looked around slowly, somehow with the manner of a man to whom any exertion at all is enormously difficult.

"What's that?"

"I was with—gang huntin' that fella," panted Jim. He seemed to sob with exhaustion. "I wasn't—strong. I— caved in. Couldn't do what my Little Fella told me! Couldn't! I fell down an' couldn't get up. . . . Passed out . . . Fainted, I guess. When I come to I was lost. . . . Tried to find the gang. . . Found a dead fella layin' on the ground. He'd been carryin' this Little Fella . . ."

A flicker of emotion passed over the lined, thin, patient face of the man on the milking-stool.

"Carryin' a Little Fella?"

"Yeah. . . . The Little Fella's sick!" panted Jim as if in a frenzy. "He's—he's alive! I know that! But he—can't tell me nothin'. . . . He just lays there. . . ."

He moved the coat-wrapped object.

"I don't know what to do!" he cried in seeming panic.

73

"I picked 'im up an' wrapped 'im warm. I' been carryin' him ever since, tryin' to find somebody . . . Nobody but another Little Fella'll know what to do! Y'can't let a Little Fella die!"

The patient eyes looked at him wearily but without doubt. Jim's tale was so unheard-of that there could be no question of plausibility. And it called upon every commanded instinct of loyalty and devotion that the Things had infused into their victims.

"I was lost!" cried Jim again, desperately. "I couldn't get here no quicker! I'm from th' city! I don't know how to find my way around out here in the sticks! Quick! I got to take him to another Little Fella who'll tell me what to do!"

The farmer half-rose, and then settled back again as if the exertion was too great.

"Ma'll show you where the Little Fella is," he said heavily. "Our folks are all off watchin' in case that killer's still around an'—our Little Fella is mighty greedy. . . She'll tell you. . ."

Jim turned and stumbled toward the house. A fierce hope stirred in him. An apology for weakness. Possibly only two people in the farm-house. But of course! The man who served the Things would reason that if Jim were a maniac as they'd been commanded to believe, he might have disguised a victim as himself only to stop all search so he might commit further crimes in the same area. After all, the evidence that he was in the city was not conclusive—merely a cryptic telephone-call. So the search could still be going on up here in the hills while the city was also combed with exhaustive care. And if the people of this house were still hunting him, with only two humans left to serve and feed the Thing—why—they might be so enfeebled that he'd be allowed to go up to the Thing alone. Because the Thing was greedy. And that would make it unnecessary for him to kill these people. . . .

He climbed heavily up the steps outside the kitchen.

He stumbled inside. A woman sat there, her flesh almost transparent with bloodlessness. She opened her eyes.

"I—got to tell the Little Fella somethin'," said Jim in the same panting desperation. "You husban' said you'd tell me—"

Disloyalty and therefore danger to a Little Fella was unthinkable to a subject. The woman, with vast exertion, pointed. A narrow stairway to the attic. Jim bounded up it, carrying the coat-wrapped object as if it were heavy and infinitely precious.

The attic was dark and hot and still. There was a smell in it, subtly horrible to Jim's nostrils. It was not the healthy, lusty smell of an animal kin to man. It was somehow the pungent odor of filth.

An infinitesimal stirring somewhere. It was the almost noiseless movement of rags and cloth. Jim's hair tried to stand on end beneath the cap that kept him sane and free.

"The man outside," said Jim unsteadily, "told me to come up here to you."

The Things could not read men's minds. They could not even know of the nearness of a man save by their own senses. Men had to come to them and report the Things the Little Fellas wished to know. But of course all men save one were slaves, so—

Jim moved toward the sound. His flesh crawled all over. He knew that the Thing was commanding him to come close. The Thing would. And it could not tell that its commands were being absorbed by Jim's cap of wire instead of by his brain. He fumbled his way toward the sound—and it was at his feet. Maybe the Thing could see in the dark. He couldn't. And he couldn't delay and he must act with the speed of thought. Faster than the speed of thought. The Thing must not be able to send out even one flashing concept of alarm—

The match in his hand flared into flame. He had an instant's awareness of yellow-lit slanting rafters, of the attic, of a trunk or two and boxes of stored possessions; of the trimly-laid brick chimney going up to the roof. And there was a box at his feet. A quite ordinary packing-box, lined with soft and shredded rags. And in it—!

Jim thrust savagely downward with the object he had made, his coats flung away by the movement. He knew an instant of the most unholy fear that any man ever experienced, when the mouth of the woven-wire trap seemed to catch on something soft and hideously yielding. He thought he'd missed. But then he flung down his whole weight, and felt the trap shake and quiver with the violent struggles of the Thing inside it. Then he worked desperately with cold sweat pouring out all over his body, until the Thing was fastened in.

When it was done he felt a horrible nausea. Of course if iron wire closely spaced could keep out the transmitted thought of even groups of Things with their minds linked together, it should keep in the transmitted thought of a single one. And this Thing was in a cage of closely-woven wire with a cover which Jim had fastened tightly with savage twistings of the wire-ends left for the purpose. It moved about in a beastly, raging panic. The cage quivered with its strugglings. And Jim sweated all over as he struck a second match to make assurance doubly sure.

He could make out the nearly shapeless blob within the wire. He examined the fastenings and twisted them more fiercely still, and then twisted even the twistings together. Once his fingers came close to the woven wire, and tiny fangs lashed out and blood dripped from his finger. But that—like the frenzied battling of a cornered rat—somehow reassured him. The Thing had not uttered a sound. Perhaps it could not. But the oozing blood-drops made him feel a normal, human superiority.

"You understand talk," he said softly. "Now remember this. I've got a pistol. None of your damned friends can control me! And if I'm stopped by their slaves the first thing I'm going to do is put a bullet through this cage

I've got you in! Picture that, my friend! A bullet through that beastly body of yours! So if you managed to tell your friends of the fix you're in before this cage closed on you—why—that's what is going to happen to you for reward!"

His clothes felt clammy from his past fear, but now he felt a curious certainty of escape.

He picked up the cage and draped his coat about it again in the dark. He fumbled his way back to the narrow stairway, guided by the faint glow that came up it. He went downstairs, and when he came out into the kitchen he carried the cage with its ghastly occupant as if it were something very precious, to be guarded with an anxious tender care. He remembered to speak with the same exhausted urgency—even greater urgency, now.

"The—Little Fella upstairs says I got to—take him to Clearfield—quick!" panted Jim. "Where c'n I get a car?"

The ghostlike woman sitting in the kitchen nodded weakly toward the door.

"Y'mean ask y' husban'?"

But Jim did not wait for an answer. He stumbled hastily out, with the same enormous pretended solicitude for the object in his arms.

The man in the barn looked heavily up at him.

"I—got to take the Little Fella to Clearfield," panted Jim again. "Your Little Fella told me— A car—"

The patient eyes turned meditative. Then the farmer said heavily, "He just—fed. He don't bother much then. I guess that's why he didn't tell me. But if he told you. . ."

He summoned strength. He stood up. He could barely walk, but he led the way with the lantern to the small building Jim had suspected was a garage.

"Car's inside," said the patient man, with an effect of uncomplaining grimness. "Here's the keys. I—hoped he'd tell you to stay here. There's only Ma an' me an'—he's greedy. I don't guess we'll last till the folks get back. . ."

Jim clamped his lips tightly on reassurance. He took

the keys and unlocked the garage. The car was a small fuel-oil-turbine job, easy to run. He put his package— which quivered a little—on the seat beside the driver's. He got in and backed out of the garage.

"Which way's Clearfield?" he demanded feverishly.

The farmer said tiredly, "Turn right an' follow the road. Don't take the left-hand fork you'll come to 'bout a mile down. That leads upstate. Go straight ahead."

"Right!" said Jim. He let his voice crack, as if frantic with anxiety over a helpless and presumably unconscious Little Fella.

He put his foot heavily on the throttle. The little car leaped ahead. He drove swiftly out to the highway where the bus from town had dumped him. He turned right. But he didn't drive straight on when he came to the left-hand fork. He took that. He headed upstate.

Miles away, he said conversationally to the quivering Thing in the iron-wire cage beside him—the Thing that had lain so long in a soft warm nest and lived on the life of subject humans, "You beasts are damned stupid! You'd only two humans to feed on, so you weakened them until they could hardly walk and couldn't think straight at all! That's why I got away with this! If you weren't so beastly greedy you might have had a chance. . . . ."

He spoke partly to reassure himself. He clung to the thought that the man and woman who had been barely able to totter about, and who had expected to die to gratify the Thing's gluttony. He clung to the thought that they mightn't die now. It would be a long time before they went up to attic without being summoned. Maybe days. With no commands imposed on them, with no greedy drain upon the fluid in their veins, they might gain some strength. Maybe, indeed, they'd be free of all servitude to any Little Fella at all, for a while.

But that was too much to hope. And his own task had just begun.

14

THE THINGS in their nests had a concept of civilization as a state it was desirable for their subjects to maintain. Civilization meant a large population of domestic animals, whether called men or other names. Animals too uncivilized to build homes could not provide soft nests for the Things to lie in. Animals which did not possess fire could not keep them luxuriously warm. Animals which lived singly could not support the Things' gluttony. It was known to all the Things that in past ages their ancestors—themselves—had lived a precarious and uncomfortable life, full of hardships. They'd had to lay in wait for wild things, and sometimes they could subdue them by their transmitted thoughts and feed bestially, and sometimes long periods went by in which there was no food. No Thing wanted to return to those old ways of life. So civilization was a state it was desirable for their subjects to have.

Each Thing had the memories of its race. When, zestfully, they gorged themselves upon the very life-stuff of their victims, and when such gorgings were often-repeated and complete, they divided. One bloated individual grew extra limbs and extra sense-organs. Presently a line of cleavage appeared about its middle. The cleavage grew deeper, while the joined-twin Thing retained all its power to hunt and feed in its own peculiar fashion. Ultimately the last adhering patch of joined pinkish skin peeled away and there were two Things, each with all the memories and all the instincts of the

79

one Thing they had been. Which, it may be, was in some sense a justification for their gluttony, because feeding satisfied not only the normal hunger of any living thing, but feeding was the means by which they reproduced.

They had intelligence of a sort, which was strictly applied to the business of existence. Since civilization among their domestic animals meant softer, warmer nests, and no need to repeat the toilsome hunting of the early days of the race, they preferred their domestic animals to be civilized. But they had no interest in civilization as such. They were supremely indifferent to anything beyond feeding, and warmth, and softness to lie upon.

To secure those luxuries they implanted a passionate loyalty and a tender affection among their subjects—emotions which to them were merely useful elements in the make-up of inferior races. They felt no loyalty, even to their own kind. But they had learned—or perhaps it was the single ancestor of all those who possessed civilized slaves who had learned—that coöperation among their kind was useful. Linked brains, however, had been useful even in the primitive days. Now they worked together because thereby they were safest and most sure of warmth and softness and the means of gluttony. But there was no affection between them, not even between newly-separated Things who before had been one individual. They knew envy and hatred and jealousy. They had every vice of which their kind was capable. But the memories of each one went back over thousands of years. They knew that it was especially wise to coöperate as long as any of the animals called men were free of their control. When all men were enslaved, then there might be horrible conflicts among them for the means of gorging themselves. They might set their slaves to the kidnapping and theft of the slaves of other Things. They might struggle horribly to secure each other's destruction so that there might be more gloating feasts. They might send nibbling thoughts to lure away the slaves of other Things. But now. . . . .

Now they lay soft and warm. Some in crude boxes in the attics of farmhouses. Some in the boiler-rooms of city apartment-houses. Some in electrically-heated nests with thermostatic controls, lined with priceless furs. They were indifferent to beauty and quality and technical perfection, to cost and rarity and to regal state. They were parasites, like lice. They gorged upon the blood that flowed in human veins. Given warmth and softness and the nourishment they craved insatiably, they cared for nothing else but their own safety. Surely they cared nothing for the lives they preyed on. . .

So they had no civilization. They had no ruler, no laws, no ambitions, no science, no instinct to progress. But they had a deadly power which had taken them from the status of lurking hunters in the jungles of a single planet, to be the bloated, gluttonous masters of two solar systems far away. A space-ship of a thriving and venturesome race had touched upon their parent world. That space-ship had carried the ancestors of these Things back to its own home. Then other space-ships had carried other Things to yet other worlds which now sank back to barbarism while the Things that had mastered them fed and fed and fed.

And now there was Earth. The Things were here. They lay in their nests and sent out their thoughts. And humans adored them because they were commanded to, and served them because they were commanded to believe that the ultimate of bliss, and thought of them tenderly because that also they had been commanded to do.

And the Things fed and fed and fed.

15

WHEN THE sun rolled up as an angry red ball, next morning, Jim was two hundred miles away. In the first direct sun-rays the grass and the tree-leaves and even the concrete roadways were wet and sparkling with dew. The webs of morning-spiders looked like jeweled veilings hung upon the bushes. The air was fresh and very fragrant, and it was such a morning as should make any man very happy to be alive.

But Jim had driven all night long, stopping only once to refuel the little car. He was very weary, but he felt that he would never be able to sleep again. Still, with the coming of dawn it was wisest for him to hide. A glance into the back-view mirror, at daybreak, convinced him that daylight driving would be impossibly dangerous. His clothes had been taken from another man, to begin with, and did not fit him properly. The wig he'd gotten from a display-dummy did not match his hair by half a dozen shades, and his wire cap was no such snug fit as he could have made with tools and a mirror to fit it by. His head was not shaped right, with the cap on it and the wig on top of that. So he'd passed quick inspection in dim light, but daylight driving was out of the question.

He hunted for a hiding-place. He drove along a broad, six-lane highway which seemed to stretch indefinitely before him through sheer forest. A single heavy truck hove in sight, moving in the opposite direction. Its aluminum hood and body glowed readily in the dawnlight. It hummed past him and dwindled to the rear. It was gone, and the road was empty again. A rabbit darted awkwardly out of the forest and onto the highway. Jim swerved automatically to avoid it. It seemed paralyzed with fear when it discovered his approach. He was wakeful, but unbelievably tired.

He saw a tiny woods-road, seemingly unused. It had been cut across by the highway and now it was growing up swiftly in saplings and underbrush. He was past it before he realized its perfection as a hiding-place. Then he braked. It was his instinct to stop, and back up, and then drive into it. He was in the act of backing along the highway when the logical course occurred to him. He sighted carefully. If another vehicle came along now, he could not risk it. But—

He backed and swerved on the concrete to the most nearly perfect line he could manage. He backed off onto the grassy shoulder, holding the steering-wheel fixed. He backed in a long smooth curve to the exit of the disused road. He backed into it. He got out once to be sure of the way. He backed the little car completely out of sight from the highway.

The Thing quivered in its covered-over cage beside the driver's seat. Jim knew with savage satisfaction that it raged. Its iron-wire cage was not luxurious. This Thing did not lie soft and warm! The iron wires would be both cold and hard. They would be harsh and uneven. The Thing would be uncomfortable and it would be bewildered, too. All during the night it must have been sending its instructions in a frantic rage, commanding its instant rescue. But the iron wires of the cage nullified all its efforts. Probably, in the end, the Thing had merely gone into a panic, far-fallen from the complacency of a creature who possessed domestic animals called men to serve it and on whom it fed, and who had lain softly in a padded nest stinking of its own beastly odor.

Jim inspected the cage with grim care. He saw little spots of dried foam where the Thing had tried to use its sharp mandibles on the iron, to cut its way out. That sign of desperation pleased him. His eyes were cold and hard as he made very, very sure that the Thing had been able to do no damage to the security of its cage.

He debated, and moved the cage to the trunk-space of the car. Locked inside there, there would be an extra barrier of iron to the broadcast of its thoughts. When he drove on again, too, there would not be even the softening effect of a seat-cushion under the cage. It should suffer such discomfort as it most hated.

He locked the trunk-space and separated the key to it from the driving-key which controlled the car. If anything should happen— But now he went back toward the highway. He raised and set upright the saplings that had been bent over by the car. Those that had been broken, he leaned toward the road. If anyone examined the tracks outside minutely, they could tell that the car had backed in. But most men would read the trail to the highway as that of a car which had come out of a disused woods-trail and onto the highway, instead of the other way about.

He returned to the driver's seat. He made sure that he had his looted pistol handy—ready to draw and use instantly. He settled back to try to rest during the daylight hours and more especially to plan his next move. He had tried to make plans all during the night. His only conceivable hope, of course, was to use the captive Thing to persuade Security of the danger facing men. Once Security was convinced, the matter would be handled with inexorable efficiency. Wire-capped Security police could land from patrol-ships near Clearfield. They could raid and search the farmhouses. The slaves of the Things, of course, would resist in passionate loyalty to their obscene masters, but a single Thing found slavering and raging in fury in its nest would prove Jim's report to the uttermost. And then—

The rest of it would be grim buisness, naturally. They'd have to make terribly sure that no Things remained alive to make slaves of men. The Things' subjects would fight despairingly, in the impassioned belief that they fought of their own will. But the Things could be destroyed, and then—sardonically—the tyranny of Security would be justified for all time because of the overwhelming peril from which it had saved humanity. Jim himself could hope for no reward. The freedom of research for which he had fought would be gone forever. The only gain would be that men would be tyrannized over by other men instead of alien monstrosities. But even that—

Jim realized the irony of the fact that he was trying to concoct a plan by which he might make Security forever invulnerable and revered. But there was simply nothing else to do .

He sat quietly in the car, weary and bitter but unable even to think of sleep while he waited for night to come again. He heard the humming of vehicles going past on the highway a hundred yards off. Traffic was beginning to roll, now that morning had come. In an hour there would be a continuous droning of turbine-motors along all the highway's length. Had he been only a little later in finding his hiding-place, he could not well have hoped to conceal himself unseen.

It was very quiet. Leaves whispered overhead. Now and again he heard small, abrupt rustling in the dry stuff on the ground. Tiny hopping birds. Squirrels, perhaps. He heard insects and bird-songs. . .

He heard something else. Sustained movements. Something or someone moving along the overgrown woods-road. He tensed and put his hand very, very quietly to the pistol in his pocket. The movement stopped, and Jim stayed motionless. There had been no more than two feet in motion. It was not a four-footed animal. It was human. It paused, surveying the car. Of course the car was motionless and looked deserted. But if this figure grew suspicious because he could tell that it had been backed into position; if he started to go away at a run. . . .

The rhythmic movements came closer. With infinite care, Jim slid himself down toward the floor-boards. His pistol was in his hand now. If he had to shoot, maybe the cars on the highway would think someone was taking a pot-shot at game out of season. . . .

Hesitating, uncertain movements. Then the figure came close. It peered into the car.

And into the muzzle of Jim's revolver.

"If you make a noise," said Jim conversationally, "I'll kill you."

He meant it. His tone carried conviction. The eyes staring into his first blazed, and then focused on the gun-barrel, and then stared back very savagely at Jim. Above those eyes, just under the hair-line, there was a long, knife-edged scar. Then a defiant voice said furiously;

"You'll have to shoot, my friend! If you damned slaves want to make sure why I'm immune to your damned Little Fellows, you'll have to try your tricks on my corpse! Go ahead and shoot, or I'll break your damned neck. . . . . ."

16

Jim did sleep, after all. An hour after he'd been ready to blow out the brains of the man who'd come up to look in the hidden car, he lay slumped and slumbering in his seat while his new companion stood guard for the two of them. But Jim twitched a little as he slept, from the effects of strain that could not yet be released. The jerkings and twitchings, too, were outward sign of dreaming.

In the dream his present waking companion was with

him, and the two of them fled nightmarishly from pursuers of whom some carried Things in their arms. The rest were dead-white, stumbling human robots, any one of whom could be pushed over like a nine-pin. But they came by thousands and millions, feebly but with a terrible persistency. The two fugitives, it seemed to Jim, performed herculean feats of flight, and they carried things which weighted them down but which they would not abandon. And ever and again they reached some gray place in which it seemed they were safe and where they began desperately to put together the things they carried. But just as the object they planned to construct began to take form, the white, stumbling figures of the slaves of the Things came shambling toward them from the darkness all about.

Then, in the dream, they seized their burdens and fled again, because it was useless to try to fight off the blood-less hordes. And besides, there were the carried Things, who gnashed tiny sharp mandibles and drove on their cohorts with soundless shrieks of rage and blood-lust.

In the dream it seemed to Jim that he sobbed with fury as he fled.

"All we've got to do," he panted bitterly as they climbed a black precipice with a wave of weary robots climbing feebly but with blind persistence after them, "all we've got to do is set this thing up. . . ."

And then, midway up the cliff, they saw a row of white faces looking down at them from the top. The Things and their slaves were waiting for them there.

Jim opened his eyes with a start. It was mid-afternoon. There was no sunlight. Heavy clouds overspread the sky. His companion was raising, by hand, the top of the car in preparation for coming rain. He nodded as Jim jerked his eyes about in instant wariness.

"You acted like your sleep wasn't too sweet," he said drily. "I sleep that way too, nowadays. I think we'll have a storm."

The first drops of rain fell as he spoke. He finished the

job of raising the top. The patter of rain upon the forest roof rose to a clattering. Then there was a rushing sound, and the noise was a minor roar. The man with the scarred forehead climbed into the car as a downpour began.

"This," he said reflectively, "will wipe out the tracks of the car coming in here, but it'll double the depth of those going out."

"I don't think it'll matter," said Jim. He added suddenly, "Twice I've dreamed that I had the answer to the Things. It was something to be made; to be put together. I was messing with thought-transmission myself, you know. That's why Security sent me off for life custody. It seems to me that each time in my dream I was concerned with causing some effect, some interference with the thought-fields the Things make—something that would neutralize those thought-fields. I know all about it in my dream and know that it would work. But I can't remember it when I'm awake."

His companion said;

"I've worked out business problems in dreams. Sometimes the answers were faintly reasonable. Once or twice they were sound. Ninety-nine times in a hundred, though, they're sheer gibberish when you look at them in daylight."

Jim's companion was a certain Miles Brandon. He had been to the city of the Things, downstate, on business. He found that some of his business associates were unwontedly pale and bloodless. One of them invited Brandon to stay at his home. All the family was pale and wore a strangely tranquil expression. After the first night of his stay there, there was an abrupt change in the manner of the family, at breakfast. They seemed to assume that Brandon knew all about something he'd never heard of. It concerned a "Little Fellow" of whom his host spoke reverently. It became alarming when all the family stared at him bewilderedly when he asked what they were talking about. But he was politely patient for a time, thought they plainly expected him to do something remarkable before he sat down to breakfast. It was something connected with the Little Fellow. But when they stared at him and plaintively asked him why he didn't go to the Little Fellow, since the Little Fellow wanted him, he lost his temper.

A doctor arrived—pale and bloodless like his host, and with the same queer expression of tranquility. He had been summoned for Brandon. Brandon, raging, started to leave. His host tried to keep him from leaving the house and the doctor insisted on giving him some injection that Brandon would not permit. It all seemed lunacy. In the end Brandon knocked down his host and brushed aside the argumentative doctor and stamped out of the house, fuming. He breakfasted at a restaurant, registered at a hotel, and sent a porter for his belongings.

Then, at his first business appointment for the day, and while he still puzzled angrily over his host's behavior, the office door opened and a man in a white coat entered, with four policemen. They tried to soothe him and persuade him to come quietly with them to another doctor. It was preposterous. He went into a rage and knocked down the white-coated man. Then the police closed in—

And he woke up in a straitjacket. He was in the psychiatric ward of the local hospital and he was an object of vast curiosity. Doctors and nurses—with tranquil faces—looked at him sympathetically. There was extraordinary contentment all about him. Then he noted that some who at one time looked a little pale but approximately normal, at another time would be white and utterly listless and incredibly weak. And they asked him questions that did not make sense. They gave him ridiculous tests. Ultimately they X-rayed him from head to foot.

That was the turning-point. He'd been in an automobile smash-up years before and his skull had been shattered. There was a metal plate supplying the place of a part of the skull-bone which had to be removed. The X-rays showed it. Then the doctors seemed to be satisfied.

They told him that he would be operated on and a plastic plate substituted for the metal one. Then—

They were very kindly. They sympathized with him. They explained why they wanted to make him normal like themselves. The Little Fellows wanted everybody to share the happiness they brought. And because people who didn't know anything about that happiness wouldn't understand, of course nobody could be allowed to know until they did share it. And Miles Brandon had heard about it, while that strange metal plate in his head kept him—so it was assumed—from being able to share it. He should have waked in his friend's house very, very happy. When the plastic plate was substituted for the metal one, he would be very, very happy. Meanwhile, of course, he had been certified insane so he wouldn't talk about the Little Fellows who wanted to make him happy like everybody else.

There'd been a time in that straightjacket when he'd doubted his own sanity, just as Jim had done. But he came to the lustily healthful conclusion that if he was insane he preferred to stay that way. His escape was a combination of pure luck and cunning, close to the insanity he was accused of. He'd been at large for eight days now, and he was half-starved and close to despair when he came upon what he thought was an abandoned car—probably a stolen one. Now he counted on the car to get him to his home town, where certainly there would be no question of his sanity! He was a well-known citizen there. He belonged to all the leading organizations, from the Country Club on down. He'd use every cent he owned to fight this—

Jim Hunt puzzled over the dream-certainty that something could be done which would prevent the spread of the Things' dominion and end it where it existed. The rain drummed on the forest roof. Intermittent heavy splashings fell on the top of the car from branches overhead. The air became saturated with moisture, and the ground became wet, and little meandering tricklings of water ran here and there beneath the trees. The sound of the rain was enough to keep even the noise of traffic on the highway from being audible, though sometimes the whine of heavy truck-tires on wet pavement could be detected.

"I could do," said Brandon angrily, "with a couple of thick rare steaks and a mound of mashed potatoes and all the trimmings! But it's only a hundred and fifty miles to my home. When we get there. . . . . But I shan't sleep until I've started some action against those Things! I know people in Security! I'll pull wires—"

Jim's thought clicked. Not on the device that would end the danger of the Things. On something else.

"I'm just wondering," he said softly, "what your family thinks? Your business started eleven days ago. They haven't heard from you. They must have made some inquiry!"

"Surely!" said Brandon vengefully. "And no doubt they've been told that I've gone off my head! I've been warned not to take chances of getting hit on the head again. They'll be told the plate got dented, and pressure on my brain has to be relieved. But when I come driving up to the door—"

"I wonder!" said Jim. "The story they've been told is pretty plausible. That danger did exist—of a blow on the head, for you. If they were told that you'd escaped while demented, and were wandering at large, they'd worry a great deal. But suppose you do turn up and explain indignantly that the doctors wanted to operate on you to make you the slave of Little Fellas? Little, non-human creatures who hide in boiler-rooms and attics and intend to rule all of humanity? What will your family think then?"

Brandon said indignantly;

"But dammit, it's true! And you'll bear me out!"

"Surely!" said Jim with quiet bitterness. "But I'm classed as a homicidal maniac with at least one murder to my credit, and it would be considered at least an eccentricity that I insist on wearing a wire cap on my head! Will your family believe that not very plausable tale of yours, backed by an implausible person like me, as against the very plausible statement of very reputable physicians explaining that there's a dent in the plate in your skull? For that matter, don't you sometimes still suspect that it's the world that's sane and we're the crazy ones?"

Brandon ground his teeth. He was a big man, and he had been beefy, and he'd possessed all the self-confidence of a man who is an important citizen. But he had not won that importance by stupidity. He saw. He looked as if he were about to roar, in his frustration. But he said suddenly;

"There's the Thing in the cage in the car-trunk!"

"Quite so," said Jim. "And the first thing any scientist on earth would do would be to get it out of the cage for examination. And it would instantly get in touch with its fellows, and they'd link their minds together for their common good. There's no distance-limit on thought! What then?"

Brandon pictured it. He and Jim had pooled their knowledge of the Things, and while Jim had gained only a little by the exchange, Brandon understood the implication of Jim's last question. He groaned.

"Then what the devil can we do?" he demanded.

Jim stared out through the rain-swept windshield of the little car, parked in a disused woods-road while the day passed.

"I've got an idea," he said slowly. "It means getting some electrical stuff. I was sentenced to life custody for fooling with transmitted thought. I know a little about it. Maybe I can do something—with certain parts. But we'll have to buy them, because if we tried stealing them we'd never find what we want, and we both need clothes and food and so we need money—or burglaries. I think it would be most efficient if we lunatics staged a hold-up tonight. It looks like it's necessary."

17

Jim's reasoning was sound. It was wiser to get money and buy essentials than try to pilfer the essentials separately. So that night Jim, who had been a promising scientist once upon a time, and Brandon who was a leading citizen in his own home town, held up a tavern just outside a little city. They marched in with handkerchiefs over their faces, overawed four customers and the bartender, and went out with the contents of the cash-register. They roared away to the southward in their car.

Half a mile away they stopped, splashed the car frantically with mud, Brandon adjusted the fuel-injector to be slightly out of phase, and then turned back and limped past the tavern they had robbed just as visiphoned police-cars arrived in a rush. They drove placidly on with their faltering motor as the squad-cars roared off in pursuit.

Then they readjusted the fuel-injector, went into the small town nearby, and parked their car near a public visi-receiver, tuned to the nearest station and listened to advertisers on the visicasts so that nobody could escape their advertising campaigns even by leaving home.

The newscast that came on in minutes told briefly of a search continuing, downstate, for a homicidal maniac whose delusions caused him to wear an iron-wire cap upon his head. He was now charged with three murders and arson. The newscast did not speak of any search for Brandon. It did not mention that Jim was known to have possessed himself of a car.

The omissions might be intentional, to lull Jim and Brandon, separately, into a feeling of false security if they listened to the 'casts. But Jim's feat of kidnapping a Thing and tricking a farmer and his wife into continued life and the loss of a car might simply not be known. Certainly the junction of Jim and Brandon wasn't likely to have been suspected. It wasn't even likely that they were credited with the holdup of a few minutes since, or that they would be. This was two hundred and fifty miles from where Jim was hunted, and far off the direct route to Brandon's home—which would be where he was looked for.

The two of them drove all night again. They spent the early part of the next morning making Brandon presentable. Before noon he went out of their hiding-place, grandly hailed an interurban bus, and went into a town some seventy-five miles from the one in which he lived. Jim Hunt bit his nails in savage apprehension for hours. Brandon couldn't be forced to talk, of course, and no one would think to question him about Jim. But it was ticklish!

He came back shortly after three. He carried neatly-wrapped parcels and he looked half-sick.

"Clothes for you," he said. "I told them they were for my boy at school. 'Hope they fit you. A suit for myself. I didn't dare change in the shop. The things you listed from the electrical place. 'Said I had a youngster who liked to tinker with such stuff. The groceries. We can eat."

Jim said, "Well?"

"I called my home town," said Brandon very quietly. "I was afraid you were right, so I didn't call my home. I called one of my employees—not too bright, but loyal. I told him I'd gotten into trouble down-state, and hinted at a woman, and that the insanity story had been started to cover me up and had gotten out of hand. I said I'd ducked out before the man who wanted to get even with me could railroad me to an insane asylum."

Jim said again, "Well?"

"My family believes in the dented-metal-plate story," said Brandon bitterly. "They've been told my delusions in detail. There are police hidden in the house to grab me if I manage to slip back, because I believe there are little non-human things who hide in boiler-rooms and attics and intend to enslave humanity! My employee mentioned them. He was suspicious until he'd referred to them and I made a show of being angry and asked him what the devil he was talking about! Now he thinks I got into trouble, pulled the insanity gag to get out, and that it got out of my control."

Jim said, "And—"

"That's all," said Brandon. "He's going to try to reassure my wife privately that I'm not insane. I told him not to, but he will! So—" His face was taut and gray. "I can't go home. If I did, they'd not only get me, but they'd take my wife along—all very plausibly—she'd insist on going—"

Jim breathed more easily.

"I was afraid you'd call your wife," he admitted, "and we'd be sunk. Now I've got a thousand-to-one chance I want to play before I take that Thing to Security. If I know Security officials, they'll be inclined to turn the Thing over to somebody who'll let it out without precautions, and while it's raising hell and started a slave-empire of its own, I'll be shipped off to life custody and my information will be referred through channels with the endorsement, 'Report made by certified homicidal maniac.' So nothing whatever will result. I'll try this trick first. Did you get the bandages?"

He changed his clothes. They ate voraciously. Brandon bandaged Jim's head and put one arm in a sling, which somehow automatically ended all likelihood of anyone suspecting him of wearing an iron cap. They drove off in broad daylight now, and as they passed through a small town Jim made a mental note of the license-plate number of a wrecked car in a garage. If he changed the plates on this car to that number it would add a little to their slender margin of safety.

A hundred miles away, Brandon bought more electrical parts. They slept again in a side-road and took turns standing watch. This night Brandon said suddenly, "That Thing in the car-trunk. You haven't fed it. Won't it die?"

"It's a blood-feeder," said Jim hardly. "Do you want to feed it? No, it won't die. Bloodfeeders have to be able to fast long times between meals. Like ticks and bedbugs. Ticks can go six months and bedbugs longer. I'm not worried about the health of the poor Little Fella just because he hasn't any human slaves!"

They had one more day's journey to the destination Jim had in mind. Toward nightfall of the next day he turned aside from any obviously useful highway and began to thread his way along an overgrown, almost-obliterated road. The little car forded streams. They went into wilderness which grew more and more pronounced. Once, they had to move a fallen tree-trunk out of the way. Just at sundown they came to a place where there were no trees or else only small ones, and where creeping vines grew over certain shapeless mounds upon the ground. The nature of the mounds was shown by a roofless, empty-windowed one-storey brick building in their midst.

"It's a sort of ghost town," said Jim without zest. "There used to be a lot of farming up here, but hydroponics and low transportation cost wiped it out. This was what they called a crossroads village. One summer when I was a kid my Scout troop camped up here. It's fallen down a lot since then but there—"—he pointed to the brick shell—"that used to be the bank. The vault's still there. We'll need it. I give myself a week. If I don't get what I want by then, I'll try the only thing that's left. But I haven't much hope of Security."

He loaded up to transfer their living aparatus to the place where they would sleep. But he left the Thing in the car-trunk. In its cage, the Thing would neither be warm, nor lie soft, nor have anything on which to feed, but Jim could feel no concern. Early the next morning he set to work to try to destroy all the power of the Things without recourse to Security.

For materials, he had some small gadgets bought in electrical shops. For laboratory, he would use the abandoned, rusty vault of a bank that had closed down thirty years before and left its building to rot. But for motive, he had the future of the human race.

18

THE REASON for the vault was that Security had detectors of thought-transmission and had believed that Jim was not the only experimenter, and had hunted—perhaps still did—for the sources of the thought-fields its detectors could demonstrate but could not analyze. The suspicions of Security officials tended to fix themselves upon persons known to be interested in basic psychology problems. Three professors of experimental psychology were arrested and their encephalographs seized by Security agents anxious to distinguish themselves in the eyes of higher-ups by zeal. A behavioristic-study laboratory was wrecked by Security police because of apparatus whose functioning was just cryptic enough to be included in high-level orders for the tracking-down of thought-transmission apparatus as dangerous to the public safety. Jim's former friends, in particular, were cajoled and threatened and their possessions searched and their private papers examined for clues. Security had found Jim Hunt defying it—and Jim Hunt was dead, of course—but the phenomena went on even after he was disposed of. So Security hunted for other experimenters who might be defying it. But the Things who did transmit thoughts were not defying Security. They were ignoring it, They lay in warm nests and gorged themselves, and grew ever more bloated and obscene. And they continued to divide and divide—and their greed increased as the changes went on—and their numbers increased, and ever more humans were subjugated to supply them with the means of gluttony. . . . .

Jim worked in the vault. It was of heavy steel, built solidly into steel-reinforced masonry, and its value as junk would not have begun to pay for the cost of taking it apart. In thirty years the building above it had rotted and the roof had collapsed, but the massive concrete about the vault had kept its shape. The great, foot-thick combinatinon door could not be closed, now, but the thinner inner doors remained. They were rust-pitted and bent, but they could be shut so that when Jim's apparatus was complete and in operation, no single trickle of its product could escape to alarm Security further.

He assembled the parts Brandon had bought for him. The transmitter itself would be relatively simple. Since a thought-field is more nearly like an electrostatic or a magnetic field than anything else, its generation is not difficult. A magnetic field, for instance, can and does extend to infinity. An electrostatic field does the same, save where it is nullified by some accidental Faraday Cage effect. But those fields cannot convey intelligence unless they are modulated. Unmodulated thought-fields are equally without effect; in fact they are not thought-fields, because thought *is* the modulation of a field. But in any case, a transmitter, as such, was simple.

The tricky part of Jim's intended device was the modulator. It would have to receive thoughts, amplify them, and impress their modulations with much greater power on the field the transmitter was to produce. And a mechanical device to receive thought is not easy to make.

Jim talked it out with Brandon as he worked. Brandon, of course had no technical training. While he waited for Jim to succeed or fail he made rabbit-snares, found small fish in a trout-stream nearby, and revolved grim schemes of his own. Sometimes he talked of those schemes. They had to do with a one-man war he proposed against the Things, if Jim's attempts should fail. He knew that they loved warm places—attic spaces hard by chimneys, boiler-rooms, and the like. He devised tricks for introducing deadly substances into those enclosures. A favorite was a simple squib of gunpowder and powdered sulphur which a furtive figure could toss into a room with its fuse lighted. It would flare suddenly into a strangling fog of sulphur-smoke in which no Thing could live. He could always tell when a Thing was present by the stench that surrounded them. . . .

But he listened as Jim talked, as much to himself as to Brandon. Talking a thing out helps to clarify one's notions.

"The field acts like high-frequency current in a wire," he explained, vexed with himself because he could not phrase it simply. "They don't travel inside a wire, but on its surface—what's called the skin effect of high-frequency conduction. A thought-field doesn't go into metal. It stays on the surface. Except iron. But it doesn't go into iron, even, unless there's iron at the focus of the field."

He waved his hand exasperatingly as he fitted two small parts together with meticulous care.

"That sounds crazy! That focus business. A thought-field is a wave-mechanics phenomenon. It acts like a wave, and it acts like a solid particle, and it probably isn't either. Like an electron, it has no position that can be fixed. There's only a probability of position. You can say that an electron is a wave-motion that's in phase with itself and is real only at one place, but you can never know where that place is. You can say a thought-field is a wave-motion that's in phase with itself at two places; where it originates, and where it's focused. In between you can know it exists, but you can't tell where it's in phase with itself, any more than you can tell where an electron is! Has that got any meaning in it at all?"

Brandon smiled rather mirthlessly.

"Damn little," he admitted.

"I'm saying you can prove there's thought being transmitted, but you can't tell where from or where to," said Jim, irritably.

"Too bad!" said Brandon. "Security would have hunted up the first of those Things to turn up—wherever they came from—if they could have tracked it down. They insisted you were talking to your friends with your gadgets, didn't they?"

"They did," said Jim savagely. "And they were sweetly reasonable and told me that if I'd snitch on my supposed confederates the conditions of my imprisonment would be a lot easier. I'd have told on the Things, all right, if I'd known about them! In fact, if I'd been let alone a little while longer I'd have had something that would handle them!"

Brandon said nothing. They'd been at the ruins of the ghost-town for days, and Jim was growing nerve-racked and jumpy as he seemed to get nowhere. His means for experiment were so primitive as to be ludicrous. The transmitter was complete except for the modulator which would give it something to transmit. The modulator would supply both the "message" and the directive which determined the second point where the message would be real. But Jim had not achieved a workable modulator which would duplicate the results he'd had before Security stepped in. He was in the position of a man with a splendidly equipped broadcasting station with no scanner or microphone to give the signal meaning. No matter how much power was put into its tubes, no meaning could be had from its signal, Jim's transmitter would send thought, but the instrument which would supply it with thought to send, in a usable form, would simply not function.

"There's nothing supernatural about the Things," said Jim, bitterly. "We send thoughts occasionally. Telepathy works sometimes. Erratically, but past the possibility of chance. You might say that we transmit at low voltage. Very low voltage. When conditions are just right, something gets through. But the Things transmit at high voltage. Like electric eels." Then he added, "There's an illustration! We make electric currents in our brains. Encephalographs pick them up and record them. They're only minute fractions of a volt. Electric eels can make up to eight hundred volts. It's no higher quality electricity than ours, just as the Things' thinking is probably no better than ours if as good. It's just high-pressure. And we can electrocute an electric eel if we want to, by using a dynamo. We should be able to wrap these things about their own beastly bellies by putting some power on the job. But—"

He went grimly back to his task.

"Exactly what are you trying, then?" asked Brandon. "Put it in words of one syllable, won't you?"

"I'm trying," said Jim bitterly, "to beat them at their own game! There was a girl named Sally. She was the slave of a Thing that I killed, later. She'd been told that she loved me, and I think she did, but she'd also been told that first of all she had to be loyal to a Thing. So she died. . . . And I talked to a farmer and his wife. They weren't young any more, and they were the only people in their house. I stole their car and the Thing in the cage that lived on them. They'd been told to be loyal to the Thing and to serve it. And they did. It was greedy and they expected to die for their loyalty, but they kept on being loyal. I want," said Jim almost shrilly, "I want to broadcast thoughts to the Things themselves! I want to tell them that they're the slaves of men! I want them to grovel like whipped puppies to the people they've ruled before—before—"

Brandon blinked at him.

"Before what?"

"Before," raged Jim, "they think of something I've thought of! There's a trick they can pull off to end everything—like that!" He snapped shaking fingers. "If it occurs to them, they can subjugate every living human being, and probably us included, in seconds flat! Damn them, they'll be invulnerable if they—think of that trick before I can beat them—"

Then, panting with fury, he went back to his work. But fury does not lead to clear thinking, nor to meticulously accurate work with inadequate equipment. Jim worked on. His results—

There weren't any.

19 ·

THE DOMINION of the Things looked no otherwise than all the rest of the world. On parts of it the sun shone, and on other parts the rain fell. Nowhere was there any sign of other than human occupancy, because the Things preferred to stay quietly and luxuriously in their nests. But a certain problem was developing. The Things reproduced by the division of their bodies into two individuals. The frequency of that reproduction was strictly controlled by the abundance of nourishment. In the mountains, where their craft had first descended, the human population was limited. A Thing took over a family and became its parasitic master. He—or It—could destroy them by unbridled demands upon their strength. Every beastly instinct urged just that. But the manner of their reproduction involved just the retention in each individual of every memory of past generations. And the Things which had subdued two solar systems to their will had been wise Things. Wisely, if reluctantly, they had curbed their appetite for gluttony until it could safely be indulged. So the Things in the mountain area restrained themselves—somewhat.

When a Thing divided, the food-supply became plainly inadequate. So each divided Thing called upon others, and they joined together with a human slave for each. Half a dozen slaves carried half a dozen Things to a house where there was no Thing. The six overwhelmed the folks there. A Thing took up its residence as master and lord. The others went on to repeat. And the taking-over of a new household meant at least one orgy of feasting without stint because there were so many fresh animals—called men—to afford the means.

That process of distribution was adequate in a rural district for a while, but it was not enough when a city was absorbed. There were hundreds of thousands of humans to be subdued and ruled and preyed upon. The Things gorged themselves in such an ecstasy of feeding as perhaps the race had hardly known before. Their pink, hairless bodies swelled and glistened with their greed. They divided—and the abundance of domestic animals was such that one Thing had hardly become two before the two were gorged and already beginning the process of becoming four. The Things, in fact, multiplied with such incredible prolificacy that there was no time—there was no space, there were no nests—in which to spread their spawning numbers.

And that made the problem. Their instincts called for quiet and warmth and solitude for feeding. Now bickerings arose among them. Envenomed accusations and petty hatreds began. There was some danger that their crowding would actually produce physical discomfort for them! So they squabbled soundlessly, sending thoughts of hate to one another. But all, of coure still impressed upon the humans the thoughts of "*nice. . . . nice. . . .*

nice. . . ." which kept their slaves exalted and submissive and perpetually conscious of an enormous happiness.

But there was bickering. It went on even in the mountain country where they had first landed on this planet. And since the Things had no civilization of their own, nor considered the building which sheltered their nests of any consequence whatever, there was no difference of pride or position among them. Yet the Things in the rural area—if only because they dared not gorge so often —tended to think a little more clearly.

The quarrels went on for a long, long time. There were no parties, because they had no politics. They were a spawning horde of strict individualists, squabbling venomously among themselves but presenting a united front toward human beings because humans were mere domestic animals and the object of the quarreling.

Then, presently, an icy thought spread among them. It was cold and utterly factual. It was the thought of a Thing—such variants arose occasionally—who began to lose the frantic lustings of his race, and thought the more lucidly in consequence. As all Things knew, the variants of this type were doomed to grow old and to atrophy like the animals on which the Things fed. But the beginning of the disease was wisdom.

The icy thought said that now was the time for the Things to cease their foolish quarrels and coöperate so that they could quarrel in perfect freedom forever after. Six of them could control any animal, flooding its mind irresistibly with thoughts that blanked out its own consciousness. Even rage or fear or fury could not protect an animal against the linked minds of six of their race. Now they were thousands. If all their minds linked together, it would not be a simple addition of power to one. It would be a multiplication of the multiple power they gained by junction of their minds.

If every Thing linked its mind to every other, there would be such a surge of energy as even their race had never used before. The whole race of men, the whole planet would become subject at one stroke. Men would come and joyfully carry them to new subjects. The machines and the whole civilization of men would combine to distribute them everywhere over the planet, each surrounded by so many adoring slaves that they could gorge and gorge and gorge without ceasing. . . . And then there would be no need for secrecy or caution or thought for the future, because every human being would be passionately loyal to the superior race of Things.

This, said the icy thought, was necessary because men were intelligent. They must be subdued because otherwise they were possibly dangerous. They should be controlled to the last individual. Now! Immediately! Before any evil befell from their intelligence!

And it would require only a single concerted effort.

The Things in their nests did not cease their feeding, nor their quiverings of beastly enjoyment as they fed. But the squabblings lessened as the promise of the icy thought sank home. Unlimited gluttony. . . .

The Things gradually ceased their mutual venom, for coöperation which would serve them all. Minds linked tentatively,—and squabbled and broke the linkage, and then linked again. . . .

20

IT WOULD NOT work. The modulator in the vault simply would not pick up thoughts to enhance and impress upon the transmitter-field. Had Jim been less wrought up; less hag-ridden by a frantic feeling of urgency, he would have seen the completely simple reason for it. But as it was he tested and re-tested his equipment, and tried every possible re-arrangement, and was forced to the bitter conclusion that some small part bought for the device was subject to a factory defect.

He was made physically ill by the conclusion that nothing could be done. He looked at Brandon, the ashen taste of defeat in his mouth. He felt ashamed, because he had taken nearly a week to make something that was no good at all—though before his arrest by Security, exactly similar apparatus had worked admirably.

"It's tough!" said Brandon. "So now you go to Security?"

Jim nodded.

"I sent them full information once," he said hopelessly, "and the local office was under the control of the Things. So nothing happened. That may be the case again. Maybe all the higher-ups are under control. I don't know. I just have to gamble."

"As a business man," observed Brandon, "I'd say you have the wrong approach. You plan to walk into a Security office, tell them and prove to them that you're an escaped Security offender, tell them you've a Thing in a wire cage, and try to tell them what it can do—"

"Yes," said Jim bitterly. "And maybe they'll let it out only in a vault, with at least some of them wearing iron caps, maybe they'll simply let it out to examine it, and it will communicate instantly with the other Things, and they'll link their minds to it and—it'll take over!"

Brandon said reflectively, "What you need is an advance publicity campaign. You're going there to sell them an idea. What you want is for them to be trying to get some information from you. Let's see what we can do to bring that about."

Jim was morosely skeptical. He felt that the transmitter he had made should work, and that the modulator should operate without difficulty. But it didn't. The fact had knocked all the self-confidence out of him. He was going ahead with the last chance he had, but there was pure panic in the back of his mind.

"I'm going to give myself up," he said grimly, "on the off-chance that I can convince them that they were right all along and that thought-transmission is dangercus. I'm not making any sacrifice. They'll put me in prison for life, but if I stay out of prison I'll spend all my life hiding with a wire cap on my head. I'd rather take the chance of accomplishing something. If you can suggest something to improve that chance, I'll take it!"

Brandon thoughtfully laid out a plan of campaign. The most horrible part of it would be letting the Thing out of its cage, but Jim agreed, savagely. In the vault it should be as much cut off from its fellows as in the cage itself, and both he and Brandon were safe against its power.

First, though, Brandon had to make a trip into the nearest town. He came back with a camera and film and writing materials. He brought back a newspaper, too— and something was happening. There were scarehead headlines.

PLAGUE SUSPECTED IN DOWNSTATE CITY!

It appeared that newsreel photographers had taken pictures of some news event in the city from which both Jim and Brandon had made precarious escapes. When the pictures were shown in the state capital, physicians noticed alarming oddities in the appearance of a considerable number of the people on the screen. The color films, of course, were completely faithful in their reproduction of flesh-tints, and doctors considered that they detected an amazing prevalence of extreme anemia —bloodlessness—among the people on the streets. In one of the newsreel shots a woman was observed to faint, and the passersby paid no attention to her at all, as if such an occurence were so common as not even to arouse interest. State health authorities saw the pictures and called the health department of the city. The official who answered the call was himself apparently in a grave physical condition, though he denied it vehemently. Examination of the health-records filed with the state health authorities had showed a sharp and sudden rise in the death-rate. But those figures were now challenged by the very men who had made them. They now insisted that the figures were wrong. They showed signs of panic.

The newspaper account said that state health officials hinted of suspicions that some not clearly identified malady had become rife in the downstate city and that its existence was being concealed. A check with recent visitors to the city in question revealed that some had noted the same condition, but that some—themselves in extremely debilitated state—denied indignantly that anything was wrong. Those who showed excessively low blood-counts were most emphatic in insisting that conditions in the downstate city were wholly normal. They had not been known to be ill before their visits to the suspected city, though, and in spite of their infuriated protests they had been removed to hospitals where bacteriological tests were in progress.

"That," said Brandon triumphantly, "looks good! Our friends the Things are going to be unmasked, eh? We'd better go on with our job, but—"

"It looks bad!" said Jim flatly. "Very bad! The state will send some men down to look things over. They'll be shown everything, including a Little Fella. And they'll come back swearing there is nothing wrong. The bad part will be that the Things may get uneasy."

"Let 'em!" said Brandon. "I'm wishing them lots worse than that!"

But Jim clamped his jaws. There was something the Things could do, if they thought of it, which would make all human effort vain. He went to the car and drew his revolver. He unlocked the car-trunk. He was savagely ready to shoot if by any chance the Thing had gotten free of its cage.

It hadn't. The trunk-space reeked horribly of the foetor
the Thing exuded. Jim was nauseated by the stench,
but he reached in and caught hold of the cage. Then he
swore.

The Thing had slashed at his fingers with its sharp
fangs. Then it slavered horribly at the scent of blood.
Jim shook with rage. He muffled the cage in his coat
and carried it into the vault. In the open air his errand
and his surroundings combined to make a strange effect.
It was near to sunset and all the world was green and
fresh and fragrant, and everything seemed clean and
wholesome. So that the Thing raging in its cage, and its
smell, and all the implications of the Thing's existence,
seemed doubly horrible.

Inside the rusted vault, Jim and Brandon closed the
inner doors, and the Thing became walled in on all sides
with solid plates of steel. Then Jim untwisted the wires
that held the cage shut.

The Thing came out, snarling voicelessly.

It was revolting to look at, even though it no longer
glistened fatly with the sustenance it had drawn from
human veins. Its bloated belly had shrunk. The pinkish,
hairless skin was flabby now. It hung in sickening folds.
The Thing had two tiny, malevolent eyes. It had a host of
tiny members to serve for legs. It had small, sharp, deadly
fangs. And it glared at them.

It was not quite so large as a football, but it was not
afraid of them. It regarded them with an extraordinary,
impatient arrogance. It hated them, to be sure, but it
was the hatred a man might feel who had been temporarily at the mercy of lower animals, at the moment
he prepared to reassert his mastery. The Thing had even
an air of conscious, raging power!

Brandon moved suddenly. He bumped into the useless
transmitter Jim had made. It started to topple, and he
caught it nervously. He set it upright and said shakily;

"The damned Thing thinks it can control us!"

Jim's eyes burned. Things like this held humans in

bondage to be fed upon. The fury he felt would have been some protection in any case, but he deliberately loosened his wire cap. He consciously and carefully let down his guard. The Thing looked at him. Stared at him. But no thoughts hammered at him or even tried insidiously to worm their way into his consciousness. The Thing was not transmitting thought. Not to him—and because of the vault's iron walls, not anywhere.

"You won't talk, eh?" said Jim with sardonic humor. "Too bad!"

Then the Thing quivered. Its defiance suddenly melted. Its pose changed. It seemed suddenly to go into a panic. It scuttled desperately here and there on legs that were too feeble to carry it with either agility or speed. It approached the closed thin iron doors. Jim contemptuously kicked it back. The tiny fangs snapped at his shoe and pierced the leather. He shook it loose and it fled before him. It fled into its cage and shrank against the farthest end.

"I think," said Jim, "that we can handle it. You get set. When you're ready I'll shake it out of its cage again."

Brandon had not actually seen a Thing before and he turned sick. As a matter of fact, the two of them at that moment were the only human beings who had ever seen a Thing without becoming subject to it, and therefore they were the only human beings to feel the instinctive repulsion, compounded equally of horror and disgust, which is the normal human reaction to a Thing. Jim had seen this one, by match-light, an instant before he rammed down the cage upon it. He had seen another, encircled by flames of his own kindling, before it died. He felt deadly hatred, but Brandon's hands shook as he set up the camera-and-flash-bulb combination he'd gone to town to get.

They took pictures. Many pictures. The Thing seemed stunned and dazed now, though they could not guess the self-evident reason. It had flashes of hysterical fury, but on the whole it was amazingly quiescent. They photographed it from every angle, at a distance and close-up, showing every detail of its body and its similitude of a face with a mere breathing-orifice in place of a nose and its unspeakably revolting apparatus for feeding. . . .

Jim booted it scornfully back into its cage.

"Plenty tame when it's helpless!" he said contemptuously. "How do the pictures look?"

Brandon was unrolling them from the camera. He'd used self-developing, self-reversing film because it would be easier to take extra shots than to make duplicate prints for their purposes. He nodded in satsfaction.

"I think they'll do!" he told him. "Nobody can look at these and think they're faked, or that the Thing that's pictured belongs on earth! Where d'you think they came from, Jim?"

"From hell," said Jim sourly. "And I want to send 'em back there."

He vengefully refastened the fastenings of the cage. He tightened the twisted wires with pliers. He felt contempt for the Thing now, which was not wise. He underestimated its intelligence and he wholly missed the actual situation in which the Thing had found itself. But he made thoroughly sure that it was as securely caged as before, and then took it out to the car-trunk again. He and Brandon lived in the vault, which was at least weather-tight.

"I'll write those letters," Jim said grimly when he came back, "whether they do any good or not."

With the tiny light at his disposal he began. There were a good number of them, and Brandon partly dictated one or two. When he was finished, he was simply doggedly resolved.

"Probably not a bit of good," he said coldly, "but I've got to try everything. . . The devil of it is, those Thing's will be worrying about being discovered, and that's bad! Hello! The transmitter's turned on. You probably threw the switch when you almost toppled it." Then he added bitterly, "Might as well smash it!"

But he didn't, though the impulse to do so was strong. And it was rather odd that he slept soundly that night. Not, of course, because he no longer had any hope. Not even because he knew how the Things could complete the conquest of all humanity if they only happened to think of something that had occured to him.

In perspective, it seems odd that he could have gone calmly to sleep after realizing that the transmitter had been turned on while the photographs were being taken.

21

A VERY famous zoölogist was hoeing deftly in his garden —he grew excellent dahlias—when his granddaughter brought him the morning mail. He beamed at her and sat down in a garden chair to look at it. A bill or two, which he regarded with disfavor. An invitation to lecture. A letter calling his attention to an article in a scientific journal, just published, and asking his opinion. A letter—

He looked blankly at the photographs. They were three-dimensional, of course, and in color. The technical excellence of the film made up for some lack of experience in the photographer. They were pictures of a—a creature. It had a horde of small limbs for locomotion, and two small malevolent eyes, and a mere breathing-orifice instead of a nose. It's feeding apparatus—

The zoölogist said, "Preposterous!"

He looked at a second photograph of the same object. It was in a different position. There were heavy veinings beneath a flabby, pinkish, hairless skin. The way in which it balanced itself on those seemingly innumerable feeble legs. . . .

The zoölogist said, "Ridiculous!"

He looked at the third picture and snorted. He did not bother to read the letter. He went back to his hoeing. But he frowned as he worked. Presently he went back to the discarded letter. He looked at the pictures again. He said vexedly, "Fiddlesticks!"

The devices by which the creature lived and moved— if it lived and moved—were not like those of any known animal. Animals did not have an odd number of legs. They did not have four joints in their limbs. They did not have mandibular fangs. Especially, they did not have such feeding apparatus.

The zoölogist threw down the photographs a second time. He went back to his hoe, but he did not pick it up. He went yet again to the pictures. They were preposterous and ridiculous and a very suitable comment on them was, "Fiddlesticks!" But they had an irrational plausibility. He observed this improbable feature. By itself it was impossible because— But the thing that made it not impossible was there! Each arrangement was unorthodox in the animal world. But each was completely consistent with every other. The zoölogist scowled. The thing was a wonderfully clever fake. Only a trained man could appreciate how wonderfully clever it was. But there must be something that would prove it a hoax . . .

He studied the pictures with concentrated attention. He grew irritated by his findings. The thing was unheard of, but it was incredibly rational. Nobody could have combined so many ingenious improbabilities so deftly. Nobody! It was not possible to create so soundly planned an impossibility!

At last he read the letter. He hesitated a long time. Then he went angrily to his visiphone and called Security.

The parasitologist looked at the pictures that had come in the morning mail. Clever. . . . There were no parasites like this, of course, but that feeding apparatus, when you looked at it carefully, was a remarkably original and well-developed idea. No creature had it, but some creature should . . . The fangs, too. A blood-feeder, of course. Hm . . . Those very curious jointed claws at the ends of the multiple legs . . . Of course, for holding on to the animal the creature fed on! Actual parasites were small, so they needed no such devices, but if a parasite were as large as this fake. . . .

It was amusing to look for flaws in the hoax. If a parasite were this large it would need . . . Hm . . . No. Not quite clever enough! Then he blinked. He'd been wrong. Quite clever enough. Cleverer than he'd thought. The difficulty was met by this. . . .

The parasitologist examined the pictures with a mounting, absorbed interest. It was fascinating. Someone was trying to put across a clever hoax, but they must have slipped somewhere . . .

Presently he was saying excitedly to himself that only a genius could have designed this model. Everything fitted perfectly, though nothing was the way any known creature was equipped . . .

Later he was saying to himself that not even a genius could have designed this model. Nobody on earth could have done so perfect a job of imagining an animal which was not like any animal on earth in any single feature. Nobody could have interrelated so many novelties so perfectly.

When he called Security, after reading the letter, his voice shook with excitement.

A celebrated biologist called Security. He said acidly that he had been given to understand that a young man named James Hunt was about to surrender himself to Security, for cause. There was reason to believe that James Hunt had information of unparalleled importance to the science of biology. He had a specimen which must be examined by a capable man. He, the eminent biologist, very urgently requested to be allowed to interview James Hunt when he had surrendered himself and before he was shipped off to Life Custody.

The Security Coördinator of Eastern Sector 5 said pompously;
"Yes. It's ridiculous, of course, but there are reports of extensive anemia in that area. If this Hunt person has actually discovered a parasite as he declares, and it is actually responsible for the anemia—why—measures must be taken at once. At once! Check these fingerprints and see if he is actually the person his letter claims. Have the photographs examined and request an estimate of the magnification. . . ."
Jim's hand showed in one of the photographs, and the size of the Thing could very readily be deduced. But the Security Coördinator of Eastern Sector 5 had simply not noticed it. Because if he had, he would have considered that Jim was trying to play a joke on him. And of course no crime could be compared to the unthinkable insolence of trying to play a joke on a Security Coördinator!

Fat Doctor Oberon, of Physchological Precautions, beamed at a letter which did not contain any photographs at all. He had been quite sure that the young man, whom he himself had sentenced to Life Custody for experimenting in a forbidden field, had had confederates. Now here was a letter from young Hunt, who had made a truly remarkable escape from Security Custody. Hunt respectfully stated that he was surrendering himself and would bring in a sample of the thought-transmitters which Security detectors had shown to be in use, but which they had not succeeded in tracking down.
Doctor Oberon beamed complacently. The young man had learned that it would not do to trifle with Security. Obviously, he expected to secure a commutation of his sentence by complete surrender and the betrayal of his confederates. But he was a dangerous character. He

would be allowed to betray his companions, of course. But so unprincipled and desperate a person amounted to a psychological hazard for the public at large. Permanent and very strict confinement would be necessary.

Doctor Oberon sighed in pious satisfaction. It was always gratifying to have the sense of duty well done which came of a peril to the public safely fore-fended. . . .

A newspaper editor growled, "What'll these cranks think of next? Who's this Hunt fella who wrote this? 'Says he escaped Security Custody and is classed as dead, but he's very much alive and here are his fingerprints. Then he sends us these pictures and says these things are alive and he's turning one over to Security? Who's Hunt?"

Somebody investigated.

"Huh! Jumped from a patrol-ship, eh? Sounds flukey. . . . Check the fingerprints anyhow. If they do check— but they won't—get a tame scientist to classify this thing— whatever it is—and tell 'im to make it dangerous for a picture spread. Get what you can on Hunt. Now, where's that sport-scandal story—"

An hour later on the visiphone, "What's that? . . . The scientist says it's alive but not terrestrial?. . . . . Don't belong in any earthly phylon? What the hell's a phylon?. . . . . He means it's something that comes from another world? Let him stick his neck out! Make him sign it! . . . . We'll play it up as famous scientist says creatures from other worlds have reached earth. One has been captured by young Hunt and is on the way to scientific circles for examination. . . . Hey! Make it intelligent! He guesses it comes from Mars! Martians have copied the guided missiles we've sent there and come back in improved models!. . . . That's the angle . . . Say, when's this guy Hunt going to turn over this creature? We've got to have some reporters covering that. . . ."

Jim Hunt drove into the state capital with his head bandaged. The bandage held the wire cap in place, and was so obvious a trick that it was noticed and instantly dismissed, whereas a patently false head of hair would have caused him to be regarded with suspicion. He halted in traffic where a sidewalk visiphone said stridently,

"*Martians on Earth! Visitors from Other Worlds Have Arrived! Specimen of Other-World Race to reach Security Today! Do they Mean War? Read the Blade! Read the Blade! Read the Blade!*"

He caught a glimpse of the visiphone screen. It showed the front page of a newspaper, and spread across the middle of the news-columns were reproductions of three of the pictures he and Brandon had taken.

But he wouldn't let himself hope. Not yet. There was that trick the Things might think of . . . He drove on grimly toward the local office of Security. So far everything looked perfect. But everything had looked perfect when he'd made the transmitter. The transmitter had failed. This might, too. It shouldn't, but if stupidity and ineptitude could spoil anything, it was certain that the lower officials in Security would manage to spoil it . . .

There were people waiting in front of Security headquarters. Newsreel men. Still-picture photographers for newspapers. A television set-up. It simply wouldn't be possible for Security to hush up his surrender and the Thing. Even if there was a policy to make the world safe by allowing nothing that was unsafe to be known or found out or searched for.

He parked the car and got out of it. He was ignored. He opened the trunk-back. He was still ignored, though some people did sniff uneasily at the pungent filthy, beastly smell that came out of it. Carrying the cage eagerly, he essayed to work his way through—

There was a rush. A small, savage knot of men formed and broke ruthlessly through the tangle of camera-tripods and wires. They leaped upon Jim. Hands clutched at his throat. Men snarled at him with the hysterical, terrible rage implanted by the Things in the minds of their subjects at however great a distance. Something struck Jim's head with terrific force. He felt the cage snatched from his hands.

Then he knew nothing.

22

HE WAS in a court-room. In Security court, which of course was not at all like other courts. The evidence had been heard in secret, which was standard Security practice lest facts be revealed which it was unwise to have publicly known—the details of an illegal experiment, for example. The sentence, however, would be public. There was still news-interest in Jim Hunt. He had made a remarkable escape from a Security patrol-ship. He was an unusually desperate and resolute offender against Security. And he had worked a very clever publicity trick. But instead of the forty or fifty reporters and photographers who had waited to watch his surrender to Security, now there were just two to hear his sentence and both were very junior and correspondingly blasé.

Doctor Oberon sat on the judicial bench and beamed complacently. He was distinctly a third-rate man and did not often have the chance to bask in so much publicity. When there was silence—and with no spectators and only two reporters and the Security Police present that did not take long—Doctor Oberon cleared his throat. He said blandly, "Having been detailed by Security to determine this case, I have heard all that the prisoner has to say. If he denies that his defense has been heard, let him speak now."

"It was heard," said Jim Hunt, raging, "by an opinionated fool!"

Doctor Oberon looked piously forgiving.

"The prisoner," he said with pained charity, "was previously sentenced to Life Custody for experiments in a forbidden subject, against the public welfare. He was detected in possession of an elaborate laboratory and in conjunction with other yet unapprehended criminals, conducting this highly dangerous research."

Doctor Oberon lectured complacently on the need for the protection of the public against dangerous knowledge.

"His sentence—which I was unfortunate enough to have to impose—was Life Custody. I urged him to reveal his confederates—"

Jim Hunt said clearly, "There were no confederates! But the Things transmit thought!"

"Now," said Doctor Oberon regretfully, "he comes before this court again. He surrendered himself under most suspicious circumstances. He had announced publicly that he had captured an alien, non-terrestrial life form. He claimed that he would deliver this life form for study and the verification of statements he would make on its delivery. He appeared, seemingly with the life form in question, at a Security office. And then a band of persons who were apparently his confederates in a hoax upon Security dashed at him, siezed the small supposed cage in which he ostensibly carried this most unlikely creature and fled. Since then, he has demanded that Security undertake an elaborate investigation of what he declares to be an invasion by extra-terrestrial creatures. He asserts that they have an entire section of this state under their —ah—hypnotic control. It is difficult to determine whether he is a deliberate imposter of extraordinary brashness, or a person subject to delusions."

Jim said bitterly, "The delusion is Security's, that you're qualified to make any decision that requires intelligence!"

But Doctor Oberon continued to be complacent.

"The decision of the court is that the prisoner has established no claim to a reconsideration of his sentence by reason of service to Security. His alleged information is either deliberate and unconvincing falsehood, or sheer delusion. This court orders that his sentence to Life Custody shall stand. However, since while at large he is alleged to have committed various crimes, including murder, this court orders that he be delivered to the criminal courts for trial under criminal charges, and returned to Security Custody for the servings of his Security sentence when or if he is released by the criminal courts."

Doctor Oberon posed for photographs. The photographers shot flash-bulb pictures of Jim. It was routine. Their paper had been caught off-base. Now, for a while, it would stoutly maintain that Jim had been railroaded; that he'd had valuable information to give to Security. But that would be only to cover up the fact that the paper had used him for a scarehead story. Ultimately, he'd be forgotten. The reporters and photographers alike know that to be the program. These pictures would go on the inside of the paper and the story, too. This was a matter of no importance at all. . . .

Jim's face was gray. In time the Things would spread over the whole world. If they thought of the trick he'd thought of first, they'd be carried over the whole world by men. Joyfully. A sickly, beaten rage filled him. Everything was useless. The earth would become a paradise for Things. Humans would till its fields half-heartedly, because their only thoughts would be the utterly contented thoughts the Things would tell them to think. Humans would delightfully serve and admire and cherish the Things that fed on them. . . .

"NICE to have wiser people from another world to tell us what to do. . . . It will be NICE TO HAVE WISE PEOPLE TO TELL US WHAT TO DO. . . . It is good that we have visitors from Mars. . . . WE WILL be glad to DO WHAT WE ARE TOLD . . . IT WILL BE GOOD TO HAVE NEW RULERS TO TELL US WHAT TO DO . . . OUR NEW RULERS ARE NICE . . . EVERYTHING IS NICE NOW THAT WE HAVE NEW RULERS . . . EVERYBOBY IS

HAPPY. . . . THE PEOPLE FROM ANOTHER WORLD MAKE EVERYBOBY HAPPY . . ."

The thoughts came into his head with crushingly convincing force, and dwindled to mere nibbling suggestions, and swelled and dwindled again as the Things established the linkage of their minds far away, and then suddenly swung into an overwhelming strength and certainty. Jim, of course, as a prisoner of Security, could no longer wear a cap of iron wire. The thoughts of thousands of Things, linked together, could not be held at bay by a single, unassisted human mind. Even rage was not enough.

He knew what was happening, but his thoughts were in a grip from which they could not escape. Uncontrollably, his mind repeated the phrases the Things sent out for all men to think.

". . . NOW ALL HUMANS WILL BE HAPPY FOR ALWAYS . . . IT IS GOOD TO OBEY THE LITTLE FELLAS. . . . WHAT THE LITTLE FELLAS TELL US TO DO IS ALWAYS WISE AND GOOD. . . . IT IS NICE TO LOVE THE LITTLE FELLAS. . . . IT IS HORRIBLE NOT TO LOVE THE LITTLE FELLAS . . . EVERYONE IS HAPPY BECAUSE THEY OBEY THE LITTLE FELLAS. . . . ONE IS HAPPY TO OBEY."

Monotonously, irresistibly, terribly, these thoughts arose in Jim's brain. They possessed a stunning intensity. The thoughts that were himself were blotted out by them. Revolt and rage were mere whispering wailings between the hammering thoughts;

" . . . . WE GO ABOUT OUR BUSINESS AND WAIT FOR THE ORDERS OF THE LITTLE FELLAS. . . . WE ACT AS USUAL, BUT WE ARE HAPPY BECAUSE THE LITTLE FELLAS TELL US WHAT TO DO. . . . WHEN WE KNOW THE LITTLE FELLAS WANT US TO DO SOMETHING, WE STOP EVERYTHING ELSE AND DO ONLY THAT. . . ."

On the judicial bench, Doctor Oberon said happily;

"It is evident that the prisoner has tried to injure our new rulers. He actually boasted that he killed one and made another a captive in a cage. So of course our duty is clear. The prisoner will be taken to our new rulers, at once, for their judgment. . . ."

It was a nightmare which Jim knew was a nightmare, but which he could not even pretend was unreal. Only, —instead of a nightmare's horror, he was filled with an insane exultation, a tragic sensation of excited happiness. Hammering thoughts pounded at him, and he knew he was going to his death or worse, but when the Security Police by his side began to lead him out of the room he went with them with his face—some remote corner of his brain knew despairingly—wreathed in a smile of utmost tranquility and peace.

He marched with them gladly while the thoughts he knew were not his own thoughts filled all his brain . . .

Then they dimmed a little. A very little more. They were muted to a mere insistent, insidious nibbling of suggestion. . . . He was being led through a corridor of iron cells. There was an iron floor underfoot. It was not enough to neutralize the thought-transmission entirely. In minds not previously conditioned by knowledge of the possibility and the horror of consciousness under outside control, the dimming of the transmitted thoughts would not even be noted. One would continue to contemplate them raptly, responding without suspicion to what seemed one's own inner consciousness.

But Jim was conditioned. Abruptly, with Security Police on either side of him, he was filled with a strangling rage and a loathing horror that blanked the intruding thoughts to whispers. He raged. He choked with fury. And his own brain took quick, grim charge. He glanced swiftly at his guards. They wore expressions of rapt inner satisfaction. They were being told that they were happy. That the Little Fellas made everybody happy. That earth was become a paradise, now that the Little Fellas were here. There was no more sorrow or grief or pain, no more poverty or want or vain striving. Everything was nice . . . nice. . . . nice. . . .

Jim spoke, steadying his voice in the effort to keep the rage out of it.

"Everybody has to do what the Little Fellas tell them," he said quietly.

The guards beside him nodded. They smiled dreamy, tranquil smiles. One does not question one's own thoughts. To the guards, the things their own minds told them seemed utterly trustworthy. One does not question one's own reasoning, one's own conclusions, one's own beliefs. The Things' transmitted thoughts seemed to have risen from within, and hence to be infallibly true; not subject to scrutiny or to question.

"The Little Fellas," said Jim as quietly as before, "don't think I'm fit to serve them. I tried to harm them. I must die."

The guards nodded again.

"Everybody obeys the Little Fellas," said Jim in a still voice. "They tell me to kill myself. Give me a pistol. It is an order of the Little Fellas. I must kill myself."

The guards looked at him numbly. But their thoughts— the thoughts they believed their own—assured them that nobody could disobey the Little Fellas. Nobody could do anything the Little Fellas did not permit. Nobody could resist or even think of resisting an order of the Little Fellas. Everyone must—

Jim reached out his hand without haste. Had he moved quickly, perhaps sheer habit would have made the guards react normally. But they were dazed by new and blinding revelation. They were absorbed in the thoughts which even Jim was still horribly aware of, here in this iron-walled, iron-floored corridor.

With tranquil certainty, Jim drew the pistol from the guard's holster. He raised it as to his own head—And struck with the raging fury of the madman he had become. The first guard reeled. Before he crashed to the floor, Jim had struck the second an equally terrible blow. He armed himself with their weapons, shaking all over with the fury he strove to make ever more overwhelming, hating so fiercely that he even allowed himself to imagine pumping bullets into the two still figures on the floor. . . .

But the Things' thoughts still came into his mind. In this corridor, and for a certain while only, he could hold at bay their cumulative influence. But his wire cap was gone. If he moved from this corridor the thoughts of the Things would again fill all his brain, driving his own thoughts and his own will down and down and out of existence. . . .

Then he saw a desk at the end of the corridor. There was an inkwell and pens on it, and a few odd papers, and a metal wastebasket beside it. Jim made a dash for the desk, panting to himself of his hatred of the Things.

At that almost he failed. The Things' thoughts filled every corner of his mind but one when he reached the desk. It was almost incredible that the pattern of action he had commanded his muscles to follow should be carried out. But it was.

Papers spilled all about him. Then he sobbed in mingled rage and relief. He had the pistols of two guards in his hands, and their cartridge-belts slung about his middle. And he was free of the Things' control. He was, at the moment, probably the only member of the human race not raptly absorbing the overwhelming rhythm of the thousands of Thing-minds, linked together.

He stood panting and raging and filled with despair, looking like a lunatic with an upside-down woven-wire wastebasket covering his head and resting on his shoulders —but the only really sane man in all the world.

23

THERE WAS probably only one hour in all of time when he could have escaped from Security Headquarters. That was the first hour of complete human submission to the Things. During that hour the Things conditioned humanity to their rule. They implanted in every human mind the rules and beliefs and habits of reaction they had found most desirable in this particular species of domestic animal. Each rule and each belief and each command to some certain reaction-pattern had to be repeated many times and in many forms. And each had to be stated and repeated with such energy that it would fill a human mind to the exclusion of all other matters at the time. So, during the first hour of their submission, humans were apt to be absent-minded. They were thinking the thoughts of the Things.

And it was during that hour that Jim went raging through the headquarters of Security with a wastebasket on his head. For safety, he added a second. He hid in a closet while he tore strips of cloth and tied both wastebaskets down to each shoulder so that by no possibility could they be knocked or fall off.

In his escape Jim shot just one man, and that man in the leg, and then only at the moment of his departure from Security Headquarters in an official Security car. That one man tried vaguely to stop him because it seemed a little remarkable even at such a time for a man wearing wastebaskets for headgear to climb into an official car and try to drive off in it.

But Jim got away. The traffic in the streets had slowed or stopped because almost everyone had ceased all activity to listen to the convincing, delightful assurances that they were very happy, happier than they had ever been before, and that earth was now a paradise because Little Fellas had come to rule it and tell humans what to do.

But when the Things in their stinking nests considered that men were conquered for all time, they broke their linkage, one by one—and fed. Only then did human activities tend to go on as usual. But they were not normal. There was an expression of unearthly tranquility on every face. The world had become transfigured. It was nice. . . . nice. . . It was paradise. Everyone was happy.

Some few humans, of course, rallied a little from even an hour-long exposure to suggestion of such intensity, possessing all the authority their own minds gave it. But those rebels were very few. Even they had had their defenses completely destroyed. Any Thing could send a thought into the mind of any one of them at any time, and any possible emotion would die at its nibbling touch to allow the thought to enter.

But Jim went raging over highways in an armed Security car with wastebaskets on his head. He was the only free man in a world of slaves to beasts. He would be hunted mercilessly by all of mankind. He must live with some such absurdity as this upon his head, and he must steal all his food. There was but one place where he was safe—in the rusty iron vault of an abandoned bank-building, on the site of a rotted-away, deserted village. His only occupation would be the hating of the Things, because he had tried to make a device which would defeat them, and had failed. Well! He would smash that first of all, to be rid of tantalizing hope. . . .

Then the Security car wobbled and almost left the road. Because in a blinding flash Jim saw again a thing that had happened.

It was a moment in the rusty vault. He'd given up the

transmitter as hopeless. Brandon was going to take some pictures of the Thing in its cage, the Thing that had been rescued by the slaves of the Things, because they knew he was going to turn it over to Security at a certain time and place.

Jim had untwisted the wires which held the cover on, and the Thing came out and glared at them. It was arrogant and furious and somehow utterly confident It was so completely confident that it was menacing, and Brandon stumbled against the useless transmitter and almost toppled it over. He'd caught it, shakily. Then he'd said, "The damned thing thinks it can control us!"

And then the Thing quivered and its defiance suddenly left it, and it appeared to go into a panic. When Jim kicked at it, it buried its fangs in his shoe, but when he shook it loose it fled back into its cage. He had to shake it out so they could take the pictures they wanted. It was cowed. *And later, he'd noticed that the transmitter was turned on!*

Driving in a speeding car that veered crazily from the shock of the discovery, Jim understood now. He understood everything that had happened. And very, very suddenly, he realized that just as the Things had had a trick with which they could enslave all humanity as soon as they thought of it, he'd had a trick that could have preserved human freedom if he'd thought of it in time, and even now could restore that freedom if only he could get back to the transmitter. . . .

He braked the car. He slowed it to the safest of speeds. He watched all traffic with a terrified fear, because a traffic accident would end the future of the human race. And he remembered the weirdness of his own appearance, with his head encased in wastebaskets, and turned the polarizing switch of the windshield and side-windows to cut down not only the light that came in, but the clarity with which anyone could see him.

And he shivered with anxiety.

When at long, long, long last he turned off a highway

and followed a disused trail into wilderness, his clothes were soaked with the sweat of terror. But he reached the open space where mounds of climbing vines lay over the ruins of what had been homes. It was night, by then, and a bright moon shone on a world of abject slaves and feasting Things.

Jim got out of the car and stumbled to the vault. It was untouched. His hands shook as he made a light and verified that the transmitter was exactly as he had left it. Brandon, doubtless, had left this hiding-place severely alone, because he was skeptical that Jim would convince Security, and if Jim were enslaved he would surely lead someone here.

Yes, everything was quite all right. He checked the batteries—those wonderful batteries of neutron-bombarded alloy which yielded power steadily for years on end. They were right. . . . .

Then thrashing sounds outside. Someone waded heavily through the underbrush. That person came to the open space which was the site of the ghost-town. He came, still stumbling, directly for the vault.

By the moonlight Jim saw who it was. Brandon. Stumbling like a drunken man. Walking with an hypnotic fixity of purpose like that of a sleep-walker. His clothes were torn by briars. He looked haggard and exhausted and dazed.

Jim stepped out into the moonlight.

"Brandon!" he said sharply. Doubt assailed him.

Brandon checked in his stride and stood swaying.

"Oh. . . Hello, Jim," he said in a sort of automaton-like precision. "You smashed it yet?"

"Smashed what?"

"That transmitter," said Brandon with the same unearthly precision. "It's got to be smashed, you know. The Little Fellas rule us now. Everybody's happy. Everybody's glad the Little Fellas tell them what to do. We have to smash everything that the Little Fellas don't like, and they don't like things that could harm them! So

I came back to smash the transmitter. Maybe it couldn't harm them, but when we made it we thought it might."

Jim stiffened.

"Funny we fought the Little Fellas," said Brandon tonelessly. "Wouldn't fight them now. I even fought them after everybody else loved 'em, Jim. But—but they kept after me. . . . —Let's smash the transmitter, Jim."

Jim plunged for him. But he stumbled, and Brandon seized him. And Brandon was a heavier man than him, and he was possessed by an hypnotic frenzy. They locked and struggled, and Jim felt bitterly that he would have to shoot his former friend, and was struggling to reach one of the pistols he had taken from his guards, when he felt Brandon tearing at the fastenings of the baskets, which held them firmly over his head.

"Listen to the Little Fellas!" said Brandon fiercely. "You're a fool to fight them! They've made everybody happy—. Look at me! When I've smashed that transmitter I'm going to find a Little Fella and tell him about it. . . ."

Then maniacal strength came to Jim. When he came to himself he was panting, and Brandon lay unconscious on the ground.

Jim dragged him into the vault and tied him fast with cords made of his own clothing. Then he took the transmitter carefully out into the open air. He turned it on. Exactly as it had been turned on at the moment they planned to take photographs and the captive Thing had suddenly turned craven and panicky.

He turned it on. That was all.

24

THE DAWN CAME. Out the open doors of the vault and through the empty space that once had been the plate-glass-windowed frontage of a bank, Jim watched a gray light steal over all the world. There were the drowsy chirpings of small birds. The light grew brighter. Ruddy sunshine smote on dew-wet grass and glistening leaves, and seemed to find all earth a place of jeweled fresh-ness. There were morning-spider webs that seemed to be made of threaded diamonds. There were spots of cob-web that looked like discs of silver on the grass.

Suddenly it was day. And Jim stood up, and loosened the absurd bonds that held his grotesque headgear to his shoulders, and walked out into the open. He put his hands to the metal baskets. He lifted them, very slowly and very cautiously at first. He took them off entirely, and seemed to listen with an intense and painful care. And then he tossed his protection away.

When Brandon opened his eyes—they were sane eyes now—Jim nodded to him, sitting bareheaded in the sun-shine. Jim looked very, very tired.

"Head clear now?" he asked heavily. "Sorry, but you wanted to smash the transmitter."

"I'm all right," said Brandon. He essayed to move, and found out his bonds. "Hm. . . . You tied me up. Good idea. —It was pretty bad, Jim. I thought I was immune. And so I was, to everything they ever shot at me before. But they pulled a new one. They put so much power into whatever they did that even I had to fight it. I held out a long time. It seemed centuries. And—I knew that if I ever stopped fighting they'd get me, and—the time came when I had to. And they did get me."

He lay still in the bonds in which Jim had tied him.

"They got everybody," said Jim. He sat quietly still.

Brandon's eyes widened suddenly.

"Hey!" he said sharply. "Where's your cap? That iron-wire cap!— Have they got you, too?"

"They haven't got anybody now," said Jim. He looked too weary to be elated. "They're licked. That's why I've thrown away my cap. It feels rather good to sit bare-headed and think that people are free. Even the ones who were conquered first of all."

Brandon's eyes were wide.

"What's that? How?"

Jim nodded listlessly at the transmitter.

"That did it. Awfully simple, after all. Remember when we were trying to make it work? I believed the transmitter was all right, but I couldn't make the modulator pick up any thoughts to feed to it. I didn't want it to retransmit the Things' thoughts! I wanted it to pick up my own. So I worked in the vault where the Things' thoughts couldn't come. And the modulator didn't pick up anything at all. Funny I didn't see it. It was so infernally simple!"

Brandon said blankly.

"I don't get it. . . ."

"I wore a wire cap to keep the Things' thoughts out of my brain. You've got a metal plate in your skull which seems to work the same way. Remember? We put a metal cage around the Thing to keep thoughts from getting out of its brain. It just didn't occur to us that we'd the same thing around ourselves. My wire cap and your metal plate kept thoughts from coming in. They also kept thoughts from going out."

Brandon said, "Oh. . . ."

"Our brains were in cages, the same as the Thing's.

So there wasn't anything in the vault for the modulator to work on. That's why it didn't work."

"But—."

"I'd taken the modulator all apart," said Jim, "and couldn't find anything wrong with it. I gave up. We got ready to take pictures. We let the Thing out. It was cocky. It tried to control us. It couldn't. We were protected. Then you stumbled against the transmitter. You caught it before it fell, and you turned it on in grabbing it. Remember we noticed it was turned on later? As soon as the transmitter went on, without modulation, the Thing got panicky. It got scared. It tried to run away. It ducked back into its cage. It was pretty tame. The transmitter did it."

Brandon, lying bound hand and foot, drew a deep breath.

"I'll take your word for it. I don't understand."

"It's just as simple as all the rest," said Jim indifferently. "Thought is the modulation of a field of force. Our brains don't make much of a field, outside our skulls, though they modulate it very well. That's why telepathy works only sometimes. The Things make a comparatively big field outside their skulls, and modulate it very well. So they can transmit thought. The transmitter yonder"—he nodded at the device—"isn't so very big, but it makes a monstrous field. And it doesn't modulate it at all."

He stopped. After an instant he shrugged and went on.

"Take a bass drum. Assume the drum-head's loose. You make a gadget that tightens it a little and taps it a little. Not much noise. Make another gadget that tightens it quite a lot and taps it pretty hard. You get a lot of noise. Then put a compressed-air line to the drum and pump in air until it's iron-hard. The air doesn't bang. But how much noise can the other gadgets make? Not much."

Brandon blinked.

"The Things make a field. They can modulate it," said Jim. "But the transmitter makes a field a thousand times

as strong. The fields blend. And the Things can't impress
a modulation on a field a thousand times as strong as
they can make! They can't drive a modulation out of
their own skulls, though their flesh, having liquid in it,
is a conductor and the field stays on the surface without
sinking in. The Things become just ordinary animals.
Incidentally, human telepathy is out of the question now,
too."

He got up and came slowly into the vault. He loosened
the bonds that held Brandon helpless. Brandon said uneasily, "D'you think it's all right to let me loose yet?"

"I think so," said Jim casually. "Anyhow I'll shoot you
if you go near the transmitter before I'm sure." Then he
smiled faintly. "I'm having too much fun to want it to
stop. I'm just picturing things to myself. Try it!"

He went out and sat down bareheaded in the sunshine again. He thought contentedly. But his thoughts
were not like those of the Things. Not at all. He
thought. . . .

There were people in the mountain country who had
a Little Fella in the attic. They waited for him to sum-
mon them, and to give them orders. Nothing happened.
They received no orders. They were not summoned.
They puzzled over it. Days passed. They ceased to wait
for commands, without realizing that they ceased to
wait. They grew stronger. They grew energetic. They
came to dread a summons to the Little Fella. Still none
came. Finally—after weeks, perhaps—someone went uneasily up to the attic. There was an evil smell there. The
Thing was still in its nest. It moved eagerly as the human drew near. But it did not order the human to approach. The someone went down shuddering a little. The
Thing was unspeakably repulsive. . . One didn't want
anything like that in the house. . . .

There was a Thing in the boiler-room of an apartment-
house in a city. It ceased to command its slaves. They

did not seek it out. Naturally! Days passed. It smelled
evily. No one went near it. It stirred eagerly when there
was movement in the cellar. But its nest was shunned.
Ultimately, in desperation, it climbed out of the nest on
its own feeble legs. Desperately, it lay in wait for a fur
naceman. When he came, it advanced upon him, slavering. He received no commands and, shuddering, moved
to avoid it. It moved desperately upon him. It sank its
fangs ravenously in his ankle. In panic, he struck it
fiercely with the coal-shovel.

He hit it. It tried to flee. He hit it again, suddenly
raging. In a frenzy of revulsion he battered it to life-
lessness.

A Thing came bumping down a flight of attic steps. It
no longer glistened fatly. Its belly was flabby and the
skin hung in folds. Its beady eyes were desperate. In the
kitchen, the woman screamed a little. The Thing moved
toward her, slavering. She ran out of the door into the
farm-yard. The Thing followed. It bumped down the
steps to the ground. A dog came toward it, bristling.
The Thing was ravenous. It was starving. It fixed its
beady eyes upon the dog, which came closer, sniffing
its foetid smell and growling. It slashed at the dog with
its fangs.

The dog tore it to pieces, snarling.

A Thing lay in a nest of soft furs, in a nest of which
the heat was thermostatically controlled. The woman who
had ordered the expensive nest prepared grew restive.
She complained to her husband of the smell. He had the
nest thrown out. The Thing was a waif. It skulked in
dark places, going mad with rage at its own helplessness
and the utter lack of response of even small, feral animals
to its will.

It tried to feed upon the kittens of an alley-cat. The
alley-cat ripped it in maternal frenzy with long sharp
claws. Suddenly blood jetted from some unprotected vein

close to its thin and hairless skin. It struggled more and more feebly. . . .

Things which were neglected. Things which were ignored. Things which were regarded at first dubiously and then disgustedly by humans who had been their slaves, and who became horribly ashamed that they had been slaves. . . . Things which were taken out-of-doors and shot because men were ashamed. . . . Things which were drowned because men hated to remember what they had done for those Things. . . . Things which had been greedy, and who were suddenly faced perhaps by the parents of a human which had been the victim of a Thing's gluttony, and those parents hated the Thing for what they had allowed it to do, took the Thing and tried with horrifying ingenuity to make it pay. . . . Things which were put into cages and dumped into trash-cans for garbage collectors to take away.

And, of course, Things who were carefully examined by scientific men who tried to understand the secret of their domination and its end. Things which were carefully killed and dissected. . . . Things which an animal-trainer tried to teach to do tricks, because he knew that they understood human speech, but which he had to kill because of their insatiable blood-lust. . . . Things which had not slaves and no civilization, and no science or art or knowledge, who had suddenly become mere animals unable even to communicate with one another. . Which strayed or escaped from the places where they had been masters, and encountered each other and fought horribly for the pure purpose of cannibalism. . . . And Things which struggled with a desperate resolution to reach the place where their space-craft had landed, and found it surrounded by men who killed them ruthlessly. . . .

And Things which were doled out small rations of the blood of slaughtered animals, given to them when they responded to the painstaking questions of scientists, and withheld when they did not.

It was two weeks before three Security cars drove carefully up to the place where there had once been a village, but where now was only the shell of a single brick building and certain mounds of rotted timbers overgrown with vines. Men in the uniform of Security officials got out. They came toward the brick shell in which the vault still stood.

Jim faced them, his hand on his revolver. But he recognized one or two of them from pictures. One in particular he recognized as the tired-faced, white-haired man who had helped make the first atomic bomb, some thirty years before, and had devoted his life ever since to the prevention of the use of other bombs and their equivalents. He was the director-general of Security, but he had none of the pomposity of his underlings.

"I think," said the white-haired man, "that you must be James Hunt. You see, we improved our detectors. When we came to our senses our detectors showed a much stronger field than had ever been registered before, and we managed to trace it."

Jim said shortly, "Hm. . You should. It isn't focused."

"Yes," said the white-haired man. "I've reviewed the file on you, Mr. Hunt. Your apparatus, which we seized, was very ingenious."

Jim said coldly, "I don't think that you came here to pay me compliments!"

The Director-General of Security said humbly, "In part I did. But also I came to tell you that you can turn off your transmitter now."

"You can turn it off," said Jim grimly, "after you kill me!"

The Director-General of Security smiled faintly.

"It doesn't matter. You see, we worked with the apparatus we seized from your laboratory. We worked out the principles involved. And we've built thirty more transmitters, all of which are working now. Yours alone took care of the Things, but it's hardly likely that all the others will go out of action at the same time. We made a large number for—security. Your vigil isn't necessary any longer. That's all."

Jim relaxed. Then he shrugged. He looked at the men who had gotten out of the three Security cars.

"I suppose," he said sardonically, "that I'm under arrest, now. I've a life sentence for breach of security, I'm charged with a murder I didn't commit, with two escapes from custody, and there's a hold-up you can bring against me. I did break the law in working on thought-transmission! But if I hadn't worked at it, I'd have had no idea how to stop it! But I did smash the Things! I've got that much satisfaction!"

Then he shrugged.

"All right," he said cynically. "I suppose I've accomplished enough for one man. I go to jail now and you can smash the transmitter if you like. I'll come quietly!"

The white-haired man smiled without mirth.

"I understand your attitude," he said gently. "But we did think we were doing the right thing. Now we know we weren't. But I did not come to arrest you, but to ask your help. We have found the space-ship in which the Things came here. They had rather manlike creatures in it with them—all dead, however. The controls were designed to be operated by those manlike creatures, and not by Things. We've forced some Things to explain, by signals. It appears that they control some nine planets in two solar systems, all of them inhabited by the same beings who had apparently built and navigated the space-ship, and on whom the Things apparently—fed."

Jim's lips tensed.

"If space-travel is possible," said the Director-General, tiredly, "Now we know that we have to have it. If Things such as came to earth control any other civilization, we have to end their empire. In short, we are going to build a space-fleet to destroy the menace the Things constitute, and it is probable that we will enter into friendly relations with the race or races we liberate from them. We are reversing our policy of—isolationism. We can do nothing else. But it may be hard for some of us to change our way of thinking."

Jim said, "Well?"

"We'd like you to accept a post with Security," said the white-haired man humbly. "If not, we'd like you to advise us. We have to change our whole outlook to—well—nearly that of the people we have considered criminals. Also we will need to equip our fleet with adequate protection against transmitted thought. We have to learn—"

"I fought against Security because it tried to make us safe by not letting us find out anything that could be dangerous. But I think we can only be safe when we know how to handle anything that can be dangerous!"

The older man looked very, very humble.

"After thirty years of thinking otherwise," he said wrily, "I admit that you seem to be right. We have to reverse our position and encourage nearly everything we have forbidden. We have to live dangerously because safety appears not to be safe." Then he added almost wistfully. "It should be very fine to be a young man now, with a chance to take part in the conquest of the stars and the planting of human colonies on the Milky Way. You see, Mr. Hunt, I'm not offering you a reward for what you've done. I'm asking you for more help. We have so much to do and we need young minds! That's what I came here for!"

Jim tried to be dignified. He didn't quite make it. He grinned. He shook hands warmly. Then he said awkwardly;

"Really, sir, an awful lot of what happened was just bull luck. I pulled some awfully stupid tricks. But if you can let me help a share in starting things off in a new direction—" He drew a deep breath. "Lord, yes! You ought to meet Brandon, by the way. Brandon! Come on out here!"

And to the Director-General of Security, who was of course the most powerful man in the world, Jim Hunt added explanatorily, "He's been keeping a sub-machine-gun on you from inside there. By the way, he isn't crazy."

Brandon came out of the bank-vault. And the Director-General of Security, the head of the organization which had the final word in all the affairs of men, murmured, "He's not crazy? That's at least refreshing."

www.ingramcontent.com/pod-product-compliance
Lightning Source LLC
Chambersburg PA
CBHW050759250626
47155CB00005B/2132